Skoob Books Publishing Ltd., London presents a new imprint:

SKOOB PACIFICA is here to disseminate Postcolonial literature of the Pacific Rim and to promote understanding between continents.

At the turn of the last century, Europe developed a penchant for novels set in lands afar which had a tendency to look **at** the colonies whereas the Post-Colonials view from within themselves, experimenting with deviation from the tradition and affirming the aesthetic of the sublime as against an aesthetic of the beautiful.

"The reality of cultural entity should be the simultaneous act of eliciting from history, mythology, and literature, for the benefit of both genuine aliens and the alienated, a continuing process of self-apprehension whose temporary dislocation appears to have persuaded many of its non-existence or its irrelevance (= retrogression, reactionarism, racism, etc.) in contemporary world reality."
Wole Soyinka, *Nobel Laureate*

"Storytelling, to the readers of a *genre* of novel, written by a particular writer for a small group of people in a large and fragmented culture, still survives in those places the English like to call the Commonwealth. This idea of narration, of the active voice is in the calypsonian as the ballad singer, the narrator, the political satirist."
Derek Walcott*, Nobel Laureate*

As the *fin-de-millenium* approaches, the colonies have a voice of their own, a new *genre* has developed. Ironically, this diachrony is written in the language of the Imperialist. Behind the facade of tropical, sandy beaches and factories of video games lies the cross-cultural and interliterary tradition of two continents.

SKOOB PACIFICA: *The Empire Writes Back!*

SKOOB PACIFICA

Joint Series Editors: Ms. C.Y. Loh & Mr. I.K. Ong

Forthcoming Winter 1993/94

Forthcoming Spring 1994

SKOOB PACIFICA No. 2001

THE
RETURN

With
An Introduction
By
Dr. C.W. Watson
Department of Social Anthropology
University of Kent at Canterbury

And

Linguistic Boundaries
By
Dr. Anne Brewster
Centre For Studies In Australian Literature
Curtin University Of Technology at Perth

By The Same Author

K.S. Maniam

THE RETURN

SKOOB BOOKS PUBLISHING
LONDON

Copyright © K.S. Maniam 1981, 1993
All Rights Reserved
The Introduction © Dr. C.W. Watson
Lingustic Boundaries © Dr. Anne Brewster
Cover Painting © Latiff Mohidin
Cover Design © William Harald-Wong
Dust Jacket Photograph © O. Don Eric Peris
First published in Malaysia/Singapore by Heinemann Asia, 1981

Published in 1993 by
SKOOB BOOKS PUBLISHING LTD.
SKOOB PACIFICA series
11A-17 Sicilian Avenue
off Southampton Row and
Bloomsbury Square
London WC1A 2QH
Fax: 071-404-4398

ISBN 1 871438 04 7

Agents:
Skoob Books (Malaysia) Sdn. Bhd.
11 Jalan Telawi Tiga
Bangsar Baru
59100 Kuala Lumpur
Tel/Fax: 603-2552686

Graham Brash (Pte) Ltd.
32 Gul Drive
Singapore 2262
Tel: 65-861 1336/862 0437
Fax: 65-861 4815

Typeset by Pearly Kok & E.K. Oon Tel: 603 407 7943
Pre Press by Syarikat R&S, Malaysia. Tel: 603 783 0975
Printed by Polygraphic, Malaysia. Fax: 603 905 1553

For
my wife Saroja,
son Ramajuna and daughter Usharani
without whose understanding and support
no writing can be done

SKOOB PACIFICA No. 2001

The Return

CONTENTS

INTRODUCTION

By

Dr. C. W. Watson

Senior Lecturer Department of Social Anthropology
University of Kent at Canterbury

In a way reminiscent of Camara Laye's classic *L'Enfant Noir*, K.S. Maniam's autobiographical novel *The Return* charts the poignant journey of self-discovery of an Indian boy growing up in Malaya and gradually moving apart from his family and immediate surroundings. In the very movement of separation he is at the same time, through education, assimilating another culture. For the boy, this culture is perceived to be more rewarding and satisfying than the one in which he lives for two related reasons. In the first place the access to a new privileged knowledge which he acquires through his gradual mastery of English enables him to bring into a more objective focus the nature of social relationships which surround him and which he is thus able to transcend. And second, the literature, and the colonial mythology which comes with it, have, at the level of escapism, the capacity to take him out of himself. Thus the education provides for him not only a tool for understanding but also a space for retreat from the world of sordid everyday reality.

The novel can, then, be very easily and enjoyably read at this level, as a *Bildungsroman* detailing the education and intellectual formation of an unusual young man with all the sorrows and triumphs of experience which characterise this genre. In its scope, however, the novel attempts more than just this reconstruction of boyhood, and although additional

subjects are not always properly or fully realised they are a
significant part of the book. Within the ostensible
description of the growth to manhood, for example, three
related themes are incorporated: a sense of history, a sense
of community and a sense of character. The first of these,
history, is conveyed almost imperceptibly. There are no
dates, no intrusive indications to the reader that there is
some deliberate intention to evoke a time and a place. We
are only occasionally made aware that the period of the
narrative falls between 1940 and 1962. The political events,
the Japanese occupation, the Emergency, Independence, are
acknowledged, but, for the boy growing up, they lack the
significance of the passing of that other time of social and
economic change. The cinema, the radio, the bicycle and
the car are some of the emblems of that latter change. Most
significant of all, however, is the extension of educational
provision, the addition of new buildings to the school and,
for the boy, the movement upwards from one level of
schooling to another, bringing at each stage a renewed
sense of achievement and at the same time a recognition of
the increasing distance from the community of origin.

It is indeed this preoccupation with recording the
distance from the community which characterises much of
the description within the narrative. It needs to be said that
this is not a romantic and sentimental evocation of
community in any way. On the contrary the representation is
starkly realistic. This is a community of Indian immigrants
dependent on a system of colonial patronage and cowed by
the circumstances of the rubber plantation economy from
which they draw their livelihood. It is a community turned in
on itself, angry, shrewish, violent, engaged in unremitting
conflict, and dominated by the seemingly arbitrary
viciousness of the menfolk. One has read descriptions of
similar communities in Zola's *Germinal* and in Lawrence's
Sons and Lovers or Jasper's *A Hoxton Childhood*. The boy

recognises himself as part of that way of life, but gradually, with the growth of wisdom, he sees how he can detach himself from it. He learns first that even within the Indian community there are divisions and separations, and that class and status are demarcated by territorial and social boundaries, which are graphically described in the novel. His first triumph over the confines of the culture into which he has been born occurs when a decision is made to stay on at school, thereby implicity announcing to the community that he is moving out of the social status to which he has been ascribed. It is an announcement which, as the narrator describes, the community is quick to acknowledge through added measures of respect and deference. Prior to this, his friends had been his neighbours' children, like Ganesh the boy from next door, but from the time of secondary school in particular, it is his English speaking classmates, of different ethnic and social backgrounds who will be his peers.

The community then is recreated in the novel but the distance which the narrator has travelled from it is reflected in the detached way in which its pettiness and misery are recorded. The same detachment is attempted in the description of individuals, but in this case the closeness which the narrator still feels to some of the characters undermines that detachment. Consequently there is a more unrestrained rendering of their extraordinary lives that gives strength to the novel. First appearing, it would seem, as foils to illustrate developments in the growing self-awareness of the narrator, these individuals quickly acquire a larger stature, first the grandmother, then the eccentric schoolteacher, Miss Nancy, and recurring characters such as the supervisor Menon and Karupi, the boy's step-mother. Above all these, however, looms the character who is for the boy the locus of his own self-appraisal, his father. It is the latter who throughout the narrative implicity controls the memory of events and determines how they are selected and recorded.

The muted chronicling of changing circumstances, the sober description of a community's style of living and the faithful representation of a set of extraordinary individuals infuse the novel with a textual richness which raises it above the level of a simple account of triumph over adversity. It certainly has its faults, mostly in terms of its structure – a frequent blurring of focus, a lack of balance between sections of the narrative – but the carefully nuanced vivid descriptions, the precise turns of phrase, the snatches of humour and the lyrical but never sentimental prose more than compensate for the imperfections of structure. It is not, ultimately the plot which gives the novel its force but that wonderfully wrought sense of kaleidoscopic life.

One final point. Observing the way in which the story shifts between a concentration on the centrality of the narrator and a description of a place, a time and its people, the alert reader might be led to ponder the ambiguity of the title. What is the "Return" which is being celebrated? An answer to the question might be that there are at least three "returns" which we can distinguish: the return of the narrator back to Malaysia and his home after years abroad in England; the return of the autobiographer to the experience of childhood which he reconstructs in the writing; and, finally, the return, in the sense of a gift, a compensation, which the son makes in the form of the published novel presented to the family for them to set against the recorded disappointments and failures along the way. All three "returns" need to be given due weight by the reader.

The growing reputation of *The Return* is much deserved, and its reappearance in this new edition some twelve years after its publication will allow new readers a rare opportunity to enter imaginatively into a certain kind of Malaysian experience which is, paradoxically perhaps, both highly specific and yet universally representative.

1

My Grandmother's life and her death, in 1958, made a vivid impression on me. She came, as the stories and anecdotes about her say, suddenly out of the horizon, like a camel, with nothing except some baggage and three boys in tow. And like that animal which survives the most barren of lands, she brooded, humped over her tin trunks, mats, silver lamps and pots, at the junction of the main road and the laterite trail. Later she went up the red, dusty path, into the trees and bushes, the most undeveloped part of Bedong. The people of this small town didn't know how she managed, but they saw her before a week passed, a settled look on her face, a firm gait to her walk.

A bit of land had been cleared beside the infrequently trodden path to the Hindu cemetery. From salvaged planks, no one knew from where, she nailed the first shelter among the many she was to design. Her three sons cowered in there most of the time.

"They were like chickens afraid of slaughter," a man who had known my grandmother when she first got to Malaysia, said, laughing.

"She was a great walker in those days. She trudged to the estates, sometimes ten miles away, a load of saris she had brought from India on her shoulders. They were soon gone. Then Letchumunan, the textile merchant, gave her a cut for peddling his goods. But your grandmother wanted to light her own lamp! And her boys had become wild fowl, dust of all Bedong on their feet," the man said, his eyes glazed with searching the past for my grandmother's image.

But she had become a tinker, the white flour sack of tools bulging on her back. The women who came to answer her calls, thought, having run out of initiative, that she had come to beg. My grandmother shook her head, refusing the glass of water or tea – she wanted work. Day after day she squatted in the common yard (the shared ground of Indian habits?) of several houses, her equipment set up. The children heralded her arrival with:

"The camel is coming! The hump is here!"

Under the ringing nickname, she bent proudly to her task. The white sack yielded a tiny stove, anvil, hammer, spatulas, rolls of copper, silver foil, aluminium, lead, and a husky bellows. The children wouldn't go away, hushed and crowded round her, waiting for a miracle.

"Bring out the pot we wanted to throw away last year!" some man jokingly called one day.

My grandmother smiled to herself and fanned the coal fire with the bellows. She held the pot handed to her against the sky.

"It was like looking at stars on a lonely night," she told me, when she recalled, in snatches, her early days.

They crowded round her, jostling each other, to witness this pale woman, head always covered with a sari border, fumble at the job. The bellows husked, the coals danced blue, the tiny hammer and spatulas flashed, crossing the morning sunlight into a mysterious pattern. A knob-like steel rod pressed and cajoled. The pot hovered, light in her hands, like a delicate butterfly over the flames. When she handed the pot back the man received it reverently. My grandmother chuckled, recalling the man's surprise.

The Indian families in Bedong, within three months, had nothing to offer except the respectful glass of tea. She ended her tinker's career and once more stood, characteristically, at the cross-roads, contemplating a new job. All her Indian skills and heritage had been depleted.

"It was like treading Indian soil once more," she commented reflectively, when she sat later on the *thinnai* of her newly-built, first real house.

For a time, she said, she went around casting away the "evil eye" from ailing children. I saw her at work, some years later, her reputation still undiminished. She would fast a whole day, then, travelling sometimes on rickety bicycles, sometimes in rattling private cars, she alighted at the house of the stricken, often in remote rubber estates. The older women in the family sometimes did the job, but didn't possess the special "touch" my grandmother had. The victim of evil forces, usually emaciated, was led into the only bedroom the family shared. Under my grandmother's gentle hands the boy squatted, trembling, on the floor. To the dust the family had collected from the four corners of the house, she added certain leaves, extracting them from her embroidered pouch. I don't know whether it was her mere presence or the ritual itself which was effective, but the boy followed us to the door, unaided, when we left. The handful of chillies, dirt, salt and leaves my grandmother had thrown into the kitchen fire crackled furiously, a sign that the possessing spirit had to flee unceremoniously!

Another event interrupted her new development. The Japanese Occupation put a stop to free movement. She reverted to farming, tending her maize, tapioca and vegetable plots. She sold the surplus, accepting bags of the almost-worthless Japanese currency. Years later our house in the hospital compound was broken into by thieves; they carted away a whole trunk of what they assumed to be hoarded Malaysian notes. The moonlight must have played a

---

thinnai – Raised, cement verandah.

ghastly joke on them as they dug their hands into piles of the *banana tree bills*. We discovered the trunk abandoned a hundred yards away, our "treasure" intact!

My grandmother barely survived the Japanese Occupation but already she had become Periathai, the Big Mother. Even her grandchildren addressed her by that name. If they didn't, they were admonished by any Indian within earshot.

I was already attending school when Periathai built that real house of hers. It had a large, cool hall, a small room and an old-fashioned, Indian cooking place. We, her grandchildren, enjoyed more the colourful entrance to this house. A double-pillared affair, it had strange stories carved on its timber faces. The carver, a man who had come from India hopeful of a well-paid job, readily accepted the small fee and lodgings Periathai offered. His trudging through a series of rejections had made him a perpetual wanderer, a dependant on his story-creating chisel. He must have put all his disappointments, nostalgia and dreams into those four pillars. The walls, thinnai and even the *kolam*-covered yard appeared insignificant. Some of the Ramayana episodes stood out with palpable poignancy: Rama challenged, bow and arrow at the ready, yet his brows lined with anxiety for the missing Sita. The sculptured, fold-like flames envelope Ravana's palace and threaten to engulf Sita's tender, shapely limbs and breasts. One pillar carried the creation of the Ganges, the cascading water stilled, another the typical, rustic look of the Indian village.

Some Fridays, when Periathai said elaborate prayers, the grandchildren were invited. We waited for her, seated on the thinnai, observing the other houses, hemmed in by

banana tree bills – Currency with banana tree emblems used during the Japanese Occupation.
kolam – Intricate designs made by Indian housewives on courtyards.

hibiscus hedges, isolated by a life of their own. The rowdier among us sprawled on the unclinging, plastered soil of the compound. Then the light dimmed and Periathai arrived with her hand-cart. She never said a word but we knew every gesture and movement of the ritual she enacted on such evenings. Preceding her to the communal bathshed, we washed ourselves reverently, then returned to the thinnai, a hushed lot.

Periathai forfeited her customary warm bath. Instead, she punished herself with cold water; we heard the slap of the water on her body resounding through the mysterious dusk. When she finally emerged she was dressed in simple, white garments, her face rubbed over with saffron paste. Her hair, let down completely, fell tapering to her knobbly waist. She was almost shy then, hardly daring to look at us. But inside the house – we had been instructed to witness, even to participate – she assumed an absorbed, impenetrable air. The complex series of events gave her no time to think.

Periathai opened one of the two tin trunks she had brought from India. Handling every object gently, she took out a statue of *Nataraja*, the cosmic dancer ringed by a circle of flame, a copper tray, a hand-woven silver-and-gold sari, bangles and a *thali*. These were laid out, Nataraja raised in the centre, on an earthen dais on the wall niche. Then she drew forth bronze tier lamps and, pouring oil from a clay container, she set them, three in number, alight. The sari, the jewelry and the idol glowed now, creating a kind of eternity around them. Periathai sat cross-legged, hair wet and in unadorned clothes before the holy niche and entered a deep contemplation. Perhaps Nataraja spoke to her of the original spirit, and her personal articles of the home she had

---

Nataraja – In Hindu mythology, the cosmic Dancer, responsible for the the creation of the Universe.

thali – Sacred, yellow thread worn by Indian brides/wives.

left behind. It was a re-immersion, a recreating of the thick
spiritual and domestic air she must have breathed there,
back in some remote district in India.

The spell broke the moment she turned and smiled at
us. We scrambled for places on the large, iron bedstead
beside which were ranged clay and copper vessels holding
strange delights. There was a kind of dried, sour meat that
tasted like stringy jelly. There were balls of puffed rice with
just the right pinch of chillie, and from another long-necked
jar came snaky bits cooked in thick treacle. We were only
given two-tooth bites of these tasty morsels, more as an
appetiser for the main meal on the thinnai. There, *vadais*,
left over from the day's sales, dhal curry filled with brinjals,
potatoes, pumpkin cubes, tomato slices and *avarakai*
(Indian legumes), were served with rice. Those of us who
had "behaved" received a teaspoonful of home-brewed ghee
to flavour the spread. Then, with only a tier lamp placed in
the centre of the most complicated kolam in the cowdung-
plastered compound, Periathai told us stories. Her voice
transformed the kolams into contours of reality and fantasy,
excitingly balanced. I felt I stood on the edge of a world I
may have known.

But this feeling came crashing down with the
proclamation of Emergency rule over certain parts of the
country. We lived under the regimented, dark sky of curfew
land. The roads looked deserted even at the times they were
opened to the public. An unshakable darkness fell over us,
every night, at eleven when all lights had to be
extinguished. During the first few weeks, strange apparitions
appeared just inside the closed door, boisterous activities
sounded in the bathroom and tins rattled. I dreamed always
of a blood-covered figure suddenly confronting me with a

---

vadais – Round, dhal cakes
avarakai – Trellis-work of Indian legumes.

blood-stained *parang*, asking for sanctuary. We lived, officially, in what was termed a "black area". This designation covered small towns and remote kampungs close to jungle fringes and foothills, perfect hiding places for communist terrorists. An English estate manager had been gorily stabbed to death in his lonely bungalow, only a few miles from Bedong. The other British planters, the handful who remained, went to their Club in Sungai Petani, escorted by the military in jeeps. Sungai Petani, my schooltown, was a "white area", that is, a communist-free region.

Periathai's carved columns and kolams were neglected. She only spent the occasional night at home. Her adopted daughter, Pakiam, merely guarded the house against thefts. Determined to keep her vadai business going, she slept on a cramped, wooden platform at the back of a provision shop. The vadais would be ready, cooked on a make-shift stove, before the town was opened to the public for two hours in the morning. Then the siren went. Periathai hurried back to the Indian provision shop to wait for the two hours of business in the afternoon. Grieved by the separation from me, she made me keep her company for a day or two. People used to look quizzically at her and a few bought her wares out of charity.

"Never let anything break your spirit," she told me, though I didn't understand her.

On rainy days the streets were even more desolate, the nights completely dark, when only phantom figures squelched on the soft ground outside the window. I learned to live within prison conditions, danger massing beyond in the familiar surroundings, freedom only a dozen miles away. During the long, sleepless nights I thought sparingly; morning was a release, not an expansion. The darkness, the siren wail and an occasional gunshot built into a monstrous

---

parang – Long-bladed knife.

fear depriving me of normal behaviour. If curfew hours were reduced, as happened sometimes, to commemorate some national event, I didn't know what to do with the extra time. Used to seeing armed men at checkpoints, I panicked when there were none.

Periathai died when the curfew was lifted for good and the military disappeared from the scene in 1958. Her fortunes reached pre-Emergency prosperity, but the lump she had always had on her shoulder had grown to the size of a clenched fist. She tried to incise it but it never "ripened". Her sons took her first to the Group Hospital and later to the District Hospital in Sungai Petani. The doctor shook his head: it was terminal cancer. Periathai shrugged the diagnosis off and continued to occupy her place at the pawnshop pillar.

Her sons had their own families, so she expanded her house, adding to it two more rooms, and bought her adopted daughter jewelry. But some inner preoccupation robbed her walk of its customary jauntiness and her expression, this-world consciousness. These spells were, initially, fleeting, isolated incidents. It was when the Town Council officials got to her that she began to lose weight. She divided her time between her vadai hand-cart and the Town Council Office, appealing for land ownership on the grounds that she had occupied that bit of land long enough to be its rightful heir.

"My many spirits roam it," she told me. "When I die I'll never stop haunting the place."

But she had no papers, only a vague belief and a dubious loyalty. The houses around hers were already being pulled down. Rafters, fallen beams and charred remains gaped like a death larger than Periathai's approaching demise whenever I went – and these occasions had grown fewer – to visit her. She refused to leave the house for fear that it might be demolished during her absence. Her

customers sometimes placed special orders with which she
kept herself busy.

The Town Council men sent her an eviction notice.

She covered her vadai hand-cart, stood it at the foot of
the large bedstead, and didn't get up for almost a week. Her
body began to waste away; her sons, their wives, and her
grandchildren were constantly in the house. But she lay, her
back turned against them, the fist-like tumour straining her
blouse.

The weeks that followed emaciated her. Periathai soon
lay, hardly rustling, like a wrinkled bamboo stem on the
voluminous sheets. The Town Council sent her another
official letter: she could stay in the house until her death.
Periathai managed a smile when I got to a strangely
deserted house that evening. She held out the envelope to
me. When I finished reading the "reprieve" she said:

"Lift me."

I hesitated. She hadn't moved from the bed for more
than a month.

"Lift me," she repeated.

I took her by the arm-pits for she was light enough,
but once on the floor she shook my hands off. Moving with
great effort she wobbled towards the shrine-niche. Pakiam
trailed behind and, obeying Periathai's unspoken
commands, pulled out the tin trunk from under the
bedstead. She took out the wedding sari, *thundu* – all
mildewed – and the thali. Laying them out on a copper tray,
she placed it before Nataraja. Under her trained fingers the
several wicks of the tier lamps sprang into life almost at
once. Periathai knelt down painfully. The incense and
camphor Pakiam burned filled the room with thick smoke.
But somehow Nataraja glowed dully. The light that fell from
the tier lamps didn't throw the tin trunk, mats, lamps and

---

thundu – Woven white cloth worn over the shirt by Indian men.

hand-cart into solid relief as it had on Periathai's ritual Fridays.

From then on she sank fast. Our parents warned us not to go near her. But we had to edge close to her to catch what she was saying. She talked with obvious effort, but talk she did, with a vague premonition, of all that her eyes had seen, her ears had heard, and to whatever her spirit had responded.

We moved in to listen to the saffron-scented, death-churned memories, stories, experiences and nostalgia. She was a child, a young girl, a new bride and a widow. There was rasping wind in her voice, cold fear, romance exalting strength and devastation. She blubbered most about the sea, crooning to it, beseeching for a safe passage with her tin trunks. Some mornings she was a freshly harvested field, smelling of stalks and turned earth. We forgot our parents' warning not to breathe in her fluid words too closely. We forgot and leaned against the curve of the land she built, now with desolating winds, now with a dark and humid soil and filled with abundant fruit. Yet it was also a land haunted by ghosts, treaded lightly by gods and goddesses, violated by murderers, where a widow went through the fire to reach a dead husband.

And now the town came to her, unable to face the empty pawnshop pillar. They streamed in continuously, stood silently at the large bedstead, stared at the covered hand-cart and, stirring themselves suddenly, went out to the kitchen, to a cup of warm tea and a plate of vadais. While she sank, while her body fluids dried up, a flow of noise and chatter built up around her. She looked out of gaunt eyes, now at this man, now at that woman, and they remembered the deft hands that had danced to a certain rhythm as she wrapped their vadais. If her body diminished, her eyes never lost their vitality. And on the morning she died, speechless, her eyes never spoke a farewell.

2

My other memories were of a lush, green countryside, cloud-striated sky, the cooking place with my mother's glistening face among the pots, and a distant shed, without walls, where my father worked. When my legs were stronger he led me there and allowed me to romp on the rich, thick grass. I moved with the shadow towards the shed until, at midday, I was cowering beside the huge water tub between the thrashing stone and the cauldron. Then my father took me home for lunch.

Left at home, I gave my mother no peace. The house had only two rooms. Half of each room was taken up by a large, wooden platform. During the day it served as table, sitting dais and a place for resting. At night mats were rolled out, coverlets found and the platforms became sprawling beds. Beneath these trestles, for lack of storing space, were pushed the tins that held rice, chillies, flour, sugar and biscuits. Inside this low, crowded interior, almost tucked away from sight, were garish tin trunks. It was the graying cloth draped over them like a shroud that attracted my attention. At the sound of tins, plates and glass jars tumbling down my mother bawled at me and dragged me out. Finally, I got to the trunks, my mother gone three houses away, and made a fascinating discovery.

Fortunately my mother wasn't within hearing distance. What a solid clatter the contents made! Brass statuettes, bronze lamps, and silver trays came cascading out. I had never seen such lamps before; the squat, kerosine containers, with a wick jutting out, were incomparable to these. Tall, three-tier lamps with multiple spouts, single, hand-worked ones, stand-lamps resembling the globe and the sun! Moulding cardboard pieces held strange patterns; greenish, square and round coins, the Chinese coffeeshop owner beyond the hospital kitchen wouldn't accept, littered the bottom of these tin trunks. My mother's return curtailed further exploration.

I needn't have worried about seeing those lamps again. They appeared all over the house one dark month that year. They flickered in the cooking place, the corners of the house, at the drains beyond and in the centre of the two rooms. Two majestic tier lamps, with a long, tapering stem, burned in the last two places. My mother gave us "palm" cakes. These were sweetened, containing green-pea mash inside and the outside covered with oil. I went from lamp to lamp turning up the wicks, and fell asleep near one of them, keeping vigil.

Later that year I witnessed my first Deepavali. Again lamps played a significant part. Besides the oil lamps already placed in strategic sections of each house, gaslights flooded the long corridor that connected all the cubicle-like houses. Goats that the long-house community had bought and reared for the occasion were slaughtered. The last bleats lingered in my mind as did the red tinge in the sky at sunset. Govindan and Thoplan pumped up the gaslights. The boys brought in the banana leaves and spread them out on the floor. Arokian and Govindan strung the goat carcasses to the rafter and started skinning them with their short, sharp knives. The air filled with a stench of raw flesh and blood. Boys caught the hunks of meat the two skinners threw at them and plumped them out on the banana leaves.

The feasting began even as the skinners scraped the fat

from the meat. Tiny slices of the fat were roasted over coal fires for the very young boys. Older ones singed the goat head, split the skull, gouged out the brain lobes and swallowed them. The goat trotters were burnt over the regular fires and dumped into the soup pot. No one ate rice that night. They spooned trotter soup into their mouths, munching the bones as they watched the mutton being apportioned. The women carried away basins and began the cooking for Deepavali. Entrails were cleaned with hot water, salt rubbed in and a spicy curry made. The unmarried girls (there were a couple to each household), made the thosais on the flat "stone" and families gobbled them throughout the night. Finally the gaslights were put out; people took their rest wherever they were. And at first cockcrow, sitting before the bronze oil lamps or kerosine ones, we were massaged with gingelly oil and sent off in pairs to the cauldron of hot water at the laundry shed. But I only remember the lamps, large, blue-tinged auras on the air, the flames burning steadily.

These festivals, together with *Thaipusam* and *Ponggal*, created a special country for us. We were inhabitants of an invisible landscape tenuously brought into prominence by the lights, mango leaves strung out over the doorways, the pilgrimages to Sri Subramanya temple in Sungai Petani on Thaipusam day, the painting of the bull horns the day after Ponggal and the many taboos that covered our daily lives. We weren't allowed out of the house between midday and two o'clock: the spirits of the dead would be about. Whenever we left for a long trip, we couldn't glance over our shoulders at the house or say, "I'm going". You had to utter: "I'm coming". With these gestures and words you ensured continued existence. One wrong move brought you

---

Thaipusam – Hindu festival of repentance.
Ponggal – First day of the first month in the Hindu Calendar.

to the gates of Neraka, hell. Neraka was evoked for us on gramaphone records. Yaman's voice – the man who led us to hell – had a hoarse, frightening tone.

How does one describe the land one lived in but never saw? It was more tangible than the concrete one we flitted through every day. Darkness gave it its true dimensions. Then it vibrated within our hearts. If we saw, perhaps through some quirk of optics, a flame beside the drain, then it was a dead pregnant woman's soul come to haunt the real world; if we heard murmurs, echoed voices among the hills, they were the chanting and tinkling of banana-tree spirits dancing in the courtyard of the night. The quick rush of water in the communal bathshed signified some unappeased soul's feverish bathing. We were hemmed into our rooms, houses, and into our minds. But for all these, there were a lot of colours in our invisible world. The gigantic figures that filled our imagination were turned out in bright togas, arms heavily braceletted, necks studded with gold and heads aureoled by intricate crowns. Fair, gentle men and women (gods and goddesses, I suppose), fought off the more scheming and brutal characters in battles that clashed over our sleeping heads. The tension between good and evil shimmered therefore like an inevitable consciousness within our heads.

We were a gentle people guided and ruled by dreams. Some of these were innocent, others as violent as the thunder and lightning that ripped the sky and destroyed a calm evening. One such bolt fell on me when I had been attending the Tamil school in Bedong for a year. My father suddenly decided to take me out of the school and enrol me in The English School, later renamed Tengku Mahkota, in Sungai Petani. Karupi, my stepmother, was largely responsible for the transfer.

My father had taken Karupi and her sister, Ragini, into the household in an act of kindness. He had promised her dying mother that he would bring them up and marry them off. But when Karupi turned eighteen, ugly rumours circulated among our neighbours. My father took her to the Civil Registry in Sungai Petani to put a stop to all the talk. The submissive, quiet young woman changed into an outgoing, worldly-wise unproclaimed ruler of the household. My mother's voice rose hardly above a whisper, and only in the kitchen.

Karupi related a dream to us one morning:

"You might have heard me shouting in my sleep last night. I had a terrible dream. It's afternoon and we're taking a nap. The house is crowded with all kinds of things: radiogram, ice-box, varnished desk, silver lamps, bedsteads, large mattresses. Ravi, who isn't napping, drinks out of a golden cup in the kitchen.

"Suddenly there's an ear-deafening noise − a cry in a foreign voice. The sleepers all sit up on their comfortable beds. A white man, wearing a coat and tie, rushes at us. There's an axe in his hand. He says terrible things in a language we don't understand. Then he starts hacking away at the things we've just acquired. We try to stop him, talking in our language. But he shakes his head and the axe splinters the beds; the cotton flies and we're almost drowned. Out of this mist the white man's face appears.

"He says, 'Send the boy to English School!'

"He points at Ravi."

I remember my father's laughter. Still chuckling, he returned to sorting the dirty clothes before going to the laundry.

Karupi had spoken one sentence of English.

"Have I used the white man's tongue before?" she said. "Your father thinks the dream is to be laughed at."

She barked at us the whole day. Then she moved from house to house retelling, enlarging and shrilling over the dream. She repeated the English sentence. The neighbours smiled at her contemptuously. Karupi returned, offended and determined. She didn't attend to my father's needs during lunch.

We were familiar with such behaviour. When my father began preparing me for the Tamil school, she had sulked. He went ahead, amused most of the time, irritated occasionally. She wouldn't co-operate. I had already begun helping her with the laundry work. I came to the lunch my mother served drenched by the sun and feeling faint. My mother sometimes went into a huff. Only when she cried to have me beside her was I excused from afternoon chores.

Karupi almost succeeded in blocking my entry into the Tamil school. She would hunt out even the most secret of hiding places where my father put away the money for the initiation ceremony. He finally gave it to Thoplan, the hospital cook and Karupi's enemy, for safe-keeping. Then she turned her attention to the goat being fattened for the occasion.

"Don't let it wander around!" she yelled from the doorway. "It might eat the wrong things and become impure."

When the goat was tethered for the night and if my father wasn't around, she slipped a five-cent coin into my palm and freed the animal.

"Chase it around until it gets tired," she said. "The meat might get fatty if it doesn't get enough exercise."

I would harrass the animal, pushing and poking it on, past the laughing neighbourhood. When my father heard about it he beat me saying I wasn't to torture animals. Karupi didn't talk to him or me for a week. Then she smiled at us in a strange, over-friendly manner.

Basked by his own dreams, my father had enlisted Murugesu's talents. Murugesu had been specially brought out from India for the Tamil school in Riverside Estate. He didn't last for more than three months. Even after two years of disillusionment in Malaysia, he retained that stimulating air of scholarship and imagination. He could make you forget you were listening to a story when he told it. This very ability destroyed his future. Young tapper-girls hung around the classroom, feigning sickness to get out of their daily tapping. The young men ganged up, accused him of seducing these girls, and had him dismissed from his teaching post. Murugesu refused to move out of his estate quarters or to defend himself. He merely went round the Indian homes coaching the children in Tamil.

He shared, wholeheartedly, my father's visions for me. Bathed, and smelling of *sireh* juice, he came punctually to the house. Karupi took an instant dislike to him. She made a clamour in the kitchen or drew away the children with embroidered tales of her hardship. But after the goat incident, she was in the front room almost all the time. Murugesu became immediately inhibited.

"Have a glass of tea, Teacher," Karupi said, ambling in.

Murugesu gazed at the glass as at some defiled object. He shook his head. But Karupi left it on a stool beside him. At the end of the lesson he asked me for a glass of water. When my father returned after delivering clothes, Murugesu hurriedly said goodbye.

Karupi re-enacted this scene for a whole week.

"Your teacher friend thinks we're unclean," she remarked to my father.

"Leave him alone," my father said.

"He insults our dignity and you turn your face away," Karupi said.

My father laughed.

On Fridays Murugesu made me carry out a *puja* at the house shrine. The Tamil Primer was placed before the

---

sireh – Leaf chewed with lime and betel nut shavings.
puja – Ritualised prayer.

picture of Saraswathi, the goddess of learning. The incense-
brazier trembled in my hands as I waved it three times
round the shrine and the book. Sometimes an abrupt grunt
came from Murugesu. I stopped the puja and looked at him.
He would nod his head at the doorway. My mother,
forgetting I was saying prayers, would have come into the
room for a towel or a *vesti*. Murugesu didn't like women in
the room while I conducted the puja. Karupi came into the
room so often that I couldn't complete the ritual that Friday.
Murugesu taught me absent-mindedly and returned home
with a distraught face. At last my father had to intervene.

"You take a stranger's side against your own wife?"
Karupi said. "How's this boy going to learn the right virtues?"

My father had to stay home on Friday evenings.

Boys of my age in that hospital compound were
mostly attending The English School in Sungai Petani. Their
fathers wore *Bose* caps, swaggered aggressively and wanted
their children to speak English. They doubted my father's
political loyalties, his need to cling to the Tamil tongue and
Indian religious practices so tenaciously. They laughed at
him; they pointed derisively at our house while buying fish
from the Chinese man who cycled in with his tin tub.

The Primer I took off the shelf-shrine every Friday
evening, after the puja, had the gloss of a mysterious, rich
world. The ornamental oil lamp, with leaf motifs, the back
domed, threw a cool band of yellow light on the cover and
my hands. The incense filled me with a sense of comfort
and wonder. On such nights my voice deepened as I reeled
off the alphabet. Murugesu looked like a god himself, pot-
bellied, remote and radiating with warmth. The night
seemed like a chamber whose walls would suddenly fall
apart and reveal a more radiant landscape. I carried some of

vesti – White cloth worn by Indian men.
Bose – Patriotic cap worn in honour of Subash Chandra Bose.

this light into my excursions into the land beyond the hospital fence, into the hidden kampung huts and the river further on. Everything seemed so clear and plausible.

Karupi had her last laugh on the day of the initiation. A large crowd had gathered in the house. Menon, the Chief Dresser and administrator, had been extended a special invitation. The air flew with speculations about my intelligence, over the incense and camphor smells. Goat *kurma* spiked the conversation and the final preparations for the ceremony. I had fasted the whole day and stood in the room, the focus of attention, trembling expectantly.

Trays of bananas, oranges and apples stood on the floor. Another contained a specially decorated coconut, the shell rubbed completely with saffron paste, a cone of husk left intact at the top, and dotted with *kumkum*. On a make-shift pedestal was smoothed out a layer of white sand. Menon arrived and, with Murugesu officiating as priest, the ceremony began. The gestures came from me with a deep sureness. Murugesu's Sanskrit chanting covered me with a vibrant sensitivity. Everything went smoothly until it came to writing the symbol for *Aum* on the white sand. While I was reciting the first few letters of the alphabet, Karupi sniggered. Then the fatal laugh struck. Though I ignored it, I couldn't make the character for "Aum" easily. I succeeded after the third time, but the unexpected, disastrous clapping made me shake violently.

The applause spread uncertainly at the beginning, then with the destructive roar of a wave. Karupi had stolen the show once more, clapping as if she were more moved by the spirit of the occasion than I. Late that night she whimpered as my father thrashed her with a rattan cane. But

---

kurma – Spicy mutton preparation.
kumkum – Red powder used as decorative dots on an Indian
    woman's forehead.
Aum – The fourth state of supreme consciousness.

the next morning my father took me on his rickety bicycle to the green building in town.

I had a wonderful time there until Karupi's dream broke into my life. Our neighbours taunted Karupi.

"Send him to English School," they said whenever they passed my house.

My father's face took on a sullen look.

Karupi went on a fast. She was still a healthy, talkative woman ten days later, when my father announced his decision to send me to The English School in Sungai Petani.

The world I had known fell apart. My walk into town – the intolerable year had to be finished – was a nostalgic, upsetting one. The Chinese constable at the railway gates, the sweet, rotting smells from the fruit stalls, the reeking drains at shop corners, all turned foreign. The thought that the sky I had known also domed over other towns, frightened me. I imagined strange assaults of crowds in unfamiliar surroundings. My trips into Sungai Petani had been rare and in my child's eyes the town was a sprawling mass of shops and wide, open fields almost touching the horizon.

Murugesu, drafted into the school begun only that year, had proved to be more than a teacher. I saw him poised and pulling us towards urgent discovery. He added the other familiar dimension to my landscape. The text-books, specially ordered from India, contained fields, jungles and characters I felt for and understood. How much of these came from Periathai's own fund of knowledge I can't gauge. Elephants, deer, snakes, mongooses, dogs and cats filled the corners of the house in the hospital compound with frightening and delightful presences. The tortoise made a slow but dignified appearance. The mongoose, though scrawny and smelly, had its attraction: it fought and killed the much-revered cobra that nearly sank its fangs into a sleeping infant. Strict loyalties were undependable, even discouraged. The lines of curving, intricate Tamil writing unfolded an excitingly unexpected and knowable world. Murugesu tied most of these stories to people and incidents we knew. These characters came alive in the shopkeepers, goldsmiths, newspaper-vendor, *chettiar* and labourer we saw daily.

What a wrench it was that first day we rode the bus to The English School! I bounced on the rattan seat all the way. The grinding, rickety red bus, a cream line across its body, disgorged us at the junction. My father hailed a trishaw and the man pedalled us uphill to the school. Under the old, tall *angsana* trees stood the fathers with their sons. The ground, littered with yellow flowers, marked off a new territory. I wandered around, dazed, brushing against the men impeccably dressed in trousers and long-sleeved shirts. Some trishaw riders had brought their sons. They smiled uncomfortably, stiff in their best clothes, beckoning the boys out of the vehicles.

The school, consisting of a single, double-storied block, impressed us with its colonial architecture. A Chinese sat at a large desk on the porch. Dressed in well-pressed pants, a thin, black tie pinned rigidly to the shirt front, he rifled through piles of papers, all the time sternly keeping curious onlookers away. The pairs of huge pillars around the porch rose monumentally towards the roof. A broad staircase led off into a corridor and gloomy, large rooms. The Chinese called, efficiently and at regular intervals, the names of the boys, and the fathers stumbled up the stairs with them.

"Ravi!"

My father flung his black cigar down and, clutching me by the hand, ascended the steps. It seemed hours, my father

---

chettiar – Commonly known as a money-lender among the Indians in
   Malaysia.
angsana – Local perennial, broad trunk, yellow flowers.

being directed a few times, before we reached the
interviewing panel. The men occupied an oblong room over
the porch. My first view of them, against the spreading
angsana branches and patches of the blue, morning sky, was
astounding. It was truly another sphere altogether. Several
men waited, like male nurses, on the white-coated
Englishman who occupied a high, rattan chair. A couple of
men guided me to another chair opposite his and I gazed at
his tomato-hued face across a desert of varnished wood. The
Englishman spoke all the time through the upper row of
yellow and glistening teeth. Then he shuffled the papers and
I was released from the confining chair.

Abruptly I found myself seated in a very silent room, at
a desk, facing a square-lined exercise book. Strange,
squiggly marks swam on the page. Other boys sat gazing at
these same signs. A fair-complexioned woman stood behind
a large desk on a platform, the clean blackboard a contrast
to her shock of raven hair. She wore a frilled skirt and a
starched blouse. We gazed at her as she mimed some
incomprehensible activity.

"Write!" she commanded.

We looked at each other, bewildered, one boy
whimpering for his father.

"Shut up!"

The voice had a raucous, imperious edge to it and,
fumbling, but with one accord, we grasped the pencil on the
groove of the desk and bent over the book. I looked at the
board and at my exercise book – both contained the same,
unfinished creatures and stiff poles. Recalling my first days
in the Tamil school, I traced over these shapes. Then,
excited by the thickening stumps, curving branches and
window frames, I pressed my pencil hard against the picture
that formed. Still, it didn't make as much sense as my first
lesson at the Tamil school. I looked to my left, beyond the
corridor, to the inaccessible trees and hills. The thick jungle

infuriated me. Determined to reduce the bloated squiggles to some meaning, I added my own lines. I had accidentally discovered the code – they were really incomplete numbers!

My triumph was short-lived. To my right, boys were moaning under the teacher's slaps!

"Keep your heads down!"

The ripple of panic reached the row beside mine. A big hulk of an Indian boy made the sound that follows a meal of rice and onion curry with plenty of asafoetida in it. For some reason I felt comfortable again. Then the air filled with a damp, pungent smell.

The teacher walked hurriedly to the boy's desk. A spluttering noise greeted her arrival. The boy stood up, his palms spread over his buttocks. Laughter filled the room. The teacher stamped her foot, held her nose and staggered to her desk. Even the offender couldn't help laughing.

"Get him out of here! Clean up the mess!" she yelled before she slumped down on the chair behind the protective desk.

The class tittered and scrambled to help. The boy, Aandy, round-faced, into which were sunk two vacant, blue eyes, smiled as he was led away. Boys surrounded him, as a Roman dignitary would be on his way to the public baths. Those who remained hunted for a pail and mop and swabbed up the splotches.

"Whew! What a smell!" the teacher whined in a high, unnatural voice.

"She no backside ah?" one of the swabbers said in Tamil.

The incident banished the clinical atmosphere from the room. A hilarious note was added to the already rowdy scene when Aandy returned, flapping, in a gardener's over-sized shorts. But Miss Nancy, the teacher, had resumed command.

"That'll do," she said sternly.

We were issued glossy books, each page containing a picture, a letter and a word. The pages were splashed with orange, gray and brown, colours that immediately awed and attracted us. They transported us into a pleasant, unreachable land. The ground we walked on was dusty or black or the paths twisted, knobbled here and there with roots. I sometimes led the occasional goat my family reared to very lush, even wild, undergrowth. You heard a wet slither through the mottled bushes, a dry snap among the entangled, deep green. I stood, my attention focused by my fright, listening to a hint of creeping, rustling, mysterious life.

"A for apple," we chorused after the teacher.

"B for boy!"

"C for cart!"

"D for Dobbin!"

"E for Ernie!"

That was all we got to that afternoon. But we were already bewildered and fascinated. Dobbin and Ernie absorbed our tiny souls. Dobbin looked like a horse but its knowing eyes disconcerted me. Tufts of fur around the hooves, thick neck and broad, hefty body gave an unpleasant impression of strength. The "boy" had reappeared as "Ernie". I scrutinised him, bending down to the desk. He had tidy, tawny hair, feet sheathed in thick shoes, and he stood gazing at a scatter of yellow flowers. His face was an outline on the page, eyes set marbles of blue. He didn't rise out of the page as Sivam, the village lout, had done in the Tamil Primer.

"Ernie, Ernie, Ernie," I chanted in a whisper all the way back home.

The sound turned on strange lights inside my mind. As the bus bounced me back towards Bedong, the dusk, a heavy mist beyond the windows, caught and echoed the squelch of the tyres. I seemed to be rushed through the cold air into a scentless, nebulous region of swirling, bright colours. The rugged harshness of the rattan seats I had been thrown by in the morning, had disappeared. When I reached home my mother's dark face had a smile I didn't recognise. My body was already encrusted with sleep as she bathed me in warm water, in the communal bathroom, the familiar insect sounds falling away into the distance. Though I had bright dreams that night, some intolerable darkness pinched at my heart.

3

Ernie exerted a considerable influence on my life that first year in The English School. Looking back now, through the haze-blotched years, I see him leaf-thin, stuck to the unfolding pages of existence on an English farm. The stodgy farmhouse stood a little removed from the yellow, straw-filled barn and the mushy ground over which Tom, the farmer, gently nudged Dobbin dragging a plough. And the earth fell into wonderful heaps of pencil shavings. Some mornings, before he trudged off to school, Ernie slipped a bunch of flowers into the grateful animal's mouth. Ernie returned as he went to school, unruffled, and his clothes spotlessly clean. While he was away, the farmhouse stood on, remote, the sky fluffy, not like ours that bleached itself to a transparent blue by midday. When Ernie came back, books tied together with a leather strap and flung over his shoulder, there was Dobbin turning with the memory of the morning towards him. He looked strangely naked, shorn of his harness and the plough. The farmer stood on the sloping trail to the house, a cob pipe in his mouth, the smoke trailing upwards to the thicker curl over the chimney.

Miss Nancy seldom slapped us now, finicky, I suspect, at the thought of touching our grimy and oily faces. She sometimes handed round scented white tissue paper out of an oblong box.

"Look at the dirt!" she said, pointing at the tissue as if it had been soiled by our blood.

We trembled before we entered the class every afternoon. Miss Nancy waited for us, a heavy ferule held menacingly, beside the shiny desk and the immaculate board. A bunch of morning glory or a flower I hadn't seen before, hung, swollen, over the side of the slim, tapering vase. She waited, her hair woven into a thick red net. We prepared for the inspection, sitting down on the wooden steps, blowing on each other's bodies but otherwise still as statues. We wiped tell-tale signs of sweat from our hands and faces just as the bell rang for the start of lessons. Dirt between the nails would have been scrupulously forced out. But Miss Nancy, with her microscopic eyes, detected an invisible grain of earth in the lines of the palm or between nail and flesh. And the ferule crashed down on the knuckles.

A boy, his shirt loosened from his shorts, was turned round. She peeked into the ear, twisting it towards the light; she ran her fingernail on the chin of the upturned face. Occasionally she lifted a few strands of hair, sniffed and dropped them hastily.

"Rotten butter!" she screamed.

The Indian boys flinched. Their mothers had smoothed down their hair with coconut oil.

"Black wires!" Miss Nancy yelled on another occasion.

The same boys had forfeited their grooming grease for the clean, lacklustre fluffy look.

On certain afternoons Miss Nancy stalked through the rows of boys, sullen and disappointed. She hadn't uncovered any dirt. But the hours raced towards an exciting evening. We kept glancing up at the impassive Miss Nancy and then at the clock. Would she give us our "treat"? Then abruptly she clapped, slammed a drawer and pulled her chair close to the desk. We gathered around her and gazed at the tableau.

Built into the confining, small wooden walls of a neat
box was the miniature land that lay beyond Ernie's farm into
which he wasn't allowed to stray. Conical trees with stiff
leaves huddled in monstrous shapes, reaching and towering
over the cottage in the corner, brightened by its tiny, latticed
windows. The cottage walls could be taken apart and Miss
Nancy often did, to reveal, disappointingly, a single room
with toy furniture. She could, at will, cover the ground with
snow (cotton stretched to transparent shreds), withered,
decaying leaves, abundant and mild-looking grass, changing
the seasons as she did the stories.

Then out of another drawer came the dolls. There
were bearded little men, a hook-nosed, hunched shrew who
rode a broom, a plastic egg painted into a human face, a
wolf distinctly resembling a rakish young man with his
pointed nose and blue, penetrating eyes. The crowning
glory of the collection was a girl in a fluffed out skirt, face
immaculately white. Her golden tresses, done into braids,
swung innocently this way and that as Miss Nancy absorbed
by her narration, twitched the controlling spine-stick
nervously. Snow White's dress materials came from Miss
Nancy's discarded wardrobe. Strangely, she resembled Snow
White sometimes, when she appeared stiff and stern before
us, her cheeks pale and dabbed with spots of red. Snow
White's rival in the doll-drawer was another girl with a
darker complexion and a mischievous look in her eyes. Her
colourful dress didn't quite fit her for she bulged at the hips
and breasts. Miss Nancy handled her as often as Snow
White, but she didn't "mother" her.

Miss Nancy's repertoire consisted of *Snow White and
the Seven Dwarfs*, *Little Red Riding Hood*, *Little Bo-Peep*,
Hansel and Gretel, *Rumpulstiltskin*, *The Boy Who Cried
'Wolf'*, *The Three Bears*, *Jack and Jill*, *Jack and the Bean
Stalk* and *Humpty-Dumpty*, who repelled her. We never
knew who Miss Nancy would use, Snow White or Little Red

Riding Hood, for any of the girl-figures in the other stories. This hesitation was only momentary, but conspicuous, earlier in the year, before she grasped Snow White firmly. But as the year progressed her uncertainty increased and Little Red, as we called her, began to dominate the tales. When the narration began slowly or faltered we knew – and we became more excited – that Little Red would slip tantalisingly into Miss Nancy's hands. Three jaded boy-dolls did duty as the masculine characters, one of them bearing only the faintest resemblance to Ernie.

The heart-chilling landscape thrilled us. Miss Nancy smothered the land with cotton-snow. It hung on the cottage in intriguing nets, crawled down the branches and rose in thick layers over the ground. The dwarfs were submerged while the girl floated through the pile-up. Snow White looked ferociously beautiful, as if her cheeks had been reddened by the struggles against the bitter, overpowering winter. She almost became Little Red. Miss Nancy's brooding face, her cold, clipped tones and the jerky manipulation of the characters penetrated and froze within us a reality I didn't understand at that time. She cajoled, snared and caught, with a ruthlessness and in so many voices that we too were drawn into whatever fascinated her.

About the time Miss Nancy introduced Snow White to us, she accelerated her campaign for cleanliness. She started innocently, mimicking – I don't know how she learned Chinese and Indian sanitary habits – the way we cleaned our teeth with rice-husk ash. She had even assembled the articles we used during our morning wash on the teacher's desk. The collection of rusty pail, milk tin dipper and even a cracked, enamel spittoon (final insult?), one afternoon in front of the class, unnerved us, the Indians. Miss Nancy wore, to keep up the farce, a faded, dotted blouse and a cheap floral sarung over her dress. The class roared with laughter.

Then the scene transformed itself. A white cloth covered the desk, a vase of flowers stood daintily at one corner. On what resembled a bathroom wall – it could have been Miss Nancy's own – hung a range of toothbrushes, a soft, pink towel and, beside the plastic sink, an almost edible cake of soap. There were back-scrubbing brushes, shower caps, nail brushes, bottles of strange-looking liquids and phials of perfume. I still wonder how she could have got all those articles up the enormous stairs and into the classroom. I never saw her with the other teachers, and the school gardeners and clerks avoided her.

We were impressed, awed and needless to say, attracted. I hadn't realised that so many accessories were needed to keep the body clean. At home I just grabbed a towel, not too long ago used by my sister, ran into the communal bathshed and sloshed myself with water. Girls kept coming in for the odd pail of water for domestic use or a man ambled in from the common toilets and, hanging his sarung or vesti on the bathroom wall as a sign of occupation, washed his bum. I wore nothing around my waist. Only later was half of the room partitioned off into a bathing cubicle with a door.

As I watched Miss Nancy up at the front, my initiation flashed into my mind. Though the central figure in the ceremony, I had felt I was the least important person in the gathering. I could have been an age-old pebble, confirmed in its existence only because they had discovered it. Murugesu's presence, the incense curling towards the smoke-glazed pictures of the gods and goddesses, joss-sticks stuck into spotted bananas, had seemed the surface of an ancient, terrestrial darkness. There was no unexpectedness. I was expected and accepted. Miss Nancy made me feel I was a discovery in myself.

Paradoxically, as Miss Nancy stood at her altar of miracles, everything or nothing seemed possible. The hot, steaming afternoon stands out in my mind now: the unmoving trees outside, the solid glass cases of books inside the room, and then, the colours of our dreams, wild before, but now given particular shapes.

Against a dark formlessness within, Miss Nancy's energy dictated patterns – suddenly the trees become wholesome and functional. They swayed, as if she had willed it, under a slight breeze. The toothbrush danced between her lips, in her mouth and over her gums. Like the tea-pot which said, "I'm a little tea-pot/Short and stout," it spoke through movement under Miss Nancy's magic touch. Closetted with her we watched (her energy bounced off the bathroom articles), and were moved by (she had discarded her mimicking gestures), the inevitability of the world. We participated.

MY father lay on his side, resting his head on his crooked arm. The children from the long-house had withdrawn from the field; the rain trees they had scrambled on, swinging, stood silent. The ground throbbed with insects under the receding heat of the day. Kerosine lamps replaced the disappearing dusk-light in some houses; in others bright gaslights hissed. Babies wailed, insistently, for the milk that would see them through to the next morning.

"You're back," my mother said, hearing me put down the canvas schoolbag.

The voice was strangely muted.

When I went to the cooking place I saw her bent over a pot, heating the curry for the night meal. The curry smelled sour, singed, and when my mother turned, her face moist with steam, she looked remote.

"My teacher wants me to buy a toothbrush," I said.

She put down the ladle on the place I had known her to for years, on a clean patch in the otherwise ash-caked, grimy cement around the fireplace. Though bewildered she mechanically wiped her hands on her *thavani* border. On the ledge, behind the stove, stood a row of bottles and tins. She wrenched the lid off one of the tins and peered inside.

"Plenty of ash here," she said.

"But, Mother, teacher wants toothpaste as well," I protested.

"If you had stayed on in the Tamil school...," she said, sighing.

I sat down and cried.

"Eh, Ravi's father, come and look at this boy!" my mother called. "Am I to cook or wipe his tears?"

He stalked in among us. He seemed suddenly huge and because tired, brutal. His cigar stank of violence. His left hand hung down at his side like a battered hoe handle. The approaching night would have split into two if he had run against it.

"Why are you crying like a woman?" he thundered.

"My teacher. . ."

"Were you beaten at school?"

"His teacher doesn't like the way we clean our teeth," my mother intervened.

I was suddenly lifted from the floor and flung against the cups, plates and jars on the kitchen table. My hip struck a stool, I wobbled, and as I fell a stinging blow removed half my face. As I was lifted again an enormous fear welled up within me. My pants felt warm and wet.

"You'll break his bones!" my mother wailed.

And I fell again, shuddering against the wall. As I blacked out I felt my mother's hands on me.

The room I woke up into the next morning was filled with people and stale breath. My father sat slumped against the corner. Karupi knelt beside me, a hot wet rag in her hands,

---

thavani – Half sari worn around the house or on informal occasions.

wiping me. My mother brought me a mug of tea hurriedly.

"Are you all right, son?" Karupi said. "You frightened all of us, lying there so still."

"Shut your evil mouth!" my father said. "Let him breathe the morning air."

He waved his hands at the women and children gathered in the room. They fled immediately. My father didn't go to the laundry that day. His face, cheek bones prominent, hovered over my feverish vision that afternoon. Karupi's presence worsened my condition. My father gestured her away. Under my mother's fumbling, rough care I began to breathe normally again. In the evening she fed me the *koay teow* soup my father had bought in town. Seeing that my body was still too bruised for me to appear at lessons, my father had a letter of excuse written by one of the hospital clerks. That evening he made me sit on the old bicycle carrier and pedalled into town.

We entered the only fashionable shop in Bedong, where prices were stiff but which stocked all kinds of goods. The Chinese in his blue drawers and white singlet shuffled up to us.

"What you want, *Ayah?*" he said politely to my father.

"My son, he goes to English school," my father said.

"Yes, yes. Very good. So going to be great scholar?" he said, running a finger through my hair.

"He wants medicine for the teeth," my father said.

The man laughed and shook his head.

"You Indian got strong, white teeth. Ha! Ha! This joke!"

My father pushed me forward.

"Gibbs," I said.

The man rubbed his stomach, beneath the rolled-up fold of the singlet, thoughtfully. He dug into a pile of the

---

koay teow – Chinese, fried noodles.

ayah – Honorific for man of high social standing.

flat, toothpaste tins, then scratched his head.

"Got everything," he mumbled, his eyes travelling over the dusty, less used shelves. "This 'Kipps', what colour outside?"

"Blue," I said. "Pink inside."

My father smiled. He hadn't heard me speak so many words of English.

"Ah, so," the man said. "High class thing. Few people use."

He stepped over the rice sacks, piles of crepe paper, rusty kerosine tins, to a cobwebbed corner of the shop. He rummaged among the bric-a-brac on an even dirtier shelf behind a thickly encrusted glass door. He blew on the gray object, then wiped it with his singlet. The compact, concave lid gleamed though the surface was scratched.

"Lucky boy, your son," he said. "Price a little more. But he be a real Englishman now."

I chose a slim, hard-bristled toothbrush and my father paid for them without a word. Then he took me to a coffeeshop. He ordered while I sat at the marble-topped table clutching the package firmly. The coffeeshop man placed a cup before me and another before him. Usually my father poured some of his coffee into the saucer and slid it to me. The man brought a plate of buttered toast. I sat stiffly on the carrier instead of prattling excitedly all the way home.

THE silence in the classroom was like glass when I returned to school. My classmates spoke, gestured and smiled at me but I had lost contact with them. During the three-day absence they had become remote. I handed my letter of excuse to Miss Nancy, fearing expulsion. As I turned away from her massive, forbidding desk she laid a hand on my shoulder.

"Sick?" she said.

I shook my head.

"Hospital?" she said again.

"Yes, Teacher," I said.

The boys laughed.

Miss Nancy mimed a patient being examined by a doctor.

I shook my head steadily throughout her act, understanding at last that she hadn't asked where I lived.

"You boys are all alike. Running away from a little sanitation," she said.

She fell back to the single-word questioning.

"Toothpaste?"

"Yes, teacher."

"Toothbrush?" she said shaking me a little.

"Yes, teacher."

"Show!" she shouted and almost shoved me down the row of desks.

I fetched the articles and Miss Nancy examined them, face impassive again.

"Return to your desk," she said at last.

The boys kept throwing conspiratorial glances at each other. They smiled over their books as they wrote after having listened attentively to Miss Nancy. She walked among them, her face relaxed, the lips parted a little. She hardly paused at my desk. I made many blunders that day and stood in the corner, a conical hat on my head. I kept hoping I could prove myself in some way all the time I faced the shiny, waxed corner of the classroom. During recess I hovered on the fringe, my classmates huddled together by some esoteric preoccupation. They threw me looks touched with reproof.

I felt more comfortable back in the classroom, Ernie among us. He had gone to visit his aunt in Glasgow. The fall in temperature crystalised everything and I saw vividly that the brown jacket, the blue mufffler and the dark overcoat made him a dwarfish man. He waited on his staid, yellowing relative like a gallant lover. She sat near the large fireplace, knitting, recalling her youth. Her tidy house, one in a row, faced a smooth, clean road. A cat rubbed, occasionally, against the hydrant only a few yards away. The silence and serenity was broken by the morning clatter of the milkman, newspaper boy and postman. In the evenings, swarthy, diligent wives tickled neighbours' red-faced babies over the fences. But this levity was quickly put away as the tall, sombre figures of the husbands approached, slim or bat-like umbrellas swinging.

Sometimes Ernie and his aunt, in a more adventurous mood, took a bus into the town centre. I enjoyed this part of Ernie's stay with his aunt: it recalled my visits to my grandmother's. They peeped into shops lined with bottles of sweets, into the warm smell of confectionaries and finally, laden with parcels, reached home, fatigued. Ernie falls asleep in front of the fire. But his aunt lifts him to his feet gently and leads him to the bathroom.

Miss Nancy clapped her book shut and thumped on the desk with her ferule. The boys left their chairs and, clutching their toothbrushes and toothpaste, lined up.

The dark, dank bathroom beside the canteen was a contrast to the one Miss Nancy had planted in our imagination. A long, cement tub, the edges chipped, ran the length of one wall. The tap dripped noisily. Half the long room was cluttered with gym equipment, and cricket pads and smelled of sweat. Miss Nancy bolted the wooden door and switched on the light, a dim bulb that hung from the rafters. The boys stood in concentric circles. I was lost, once more at the fringe.

Miss Nancy demonstrated.

One by one the boys stepped forward and imitated her actions. She patted some boys and made others repeat the brushing movements. The room filled with the smell of toothpaste. I was so nervous, when it came to my turn, I couldn't open the toothpaste tin.

"Bring it here, Ravi!" Miss Nancy commanded.

With a flick of her nails she had it open. Then she held my neck and brushed my teeth. The boys giggled at such helplessness; my gums smarted.

"That's how you do it!" Miss Nancy said.

The boys marched jauntily back. Miss Nancy looked slightly dishevelled. I cringed at the back. We re-entered the classroom smelling cleaner. Miss Nancy pulled out the drawer of dolls and English country. Her hand selected Snow White quickly, purposefully, and we were launched into the story.

Miss Nancy had recovered her vigour. Her hands caressing the dress, golden hair and fragile figure of Snow White, she transformed her into a tidy housewife. Snow White floated through the house opening windows and doors, letting the air in. She moved, Miss Nancy's words flew, the dust rose and disappeared, the house shone. She turned away the dwarfs who brought in a dead rabbit or a bit of flower to please her.

"Where are your manners?" Snow White said, her fair face clouding.

"Oh, my house is all dirtied!" she cried and sat down in anguish.

The dwarfs crowded round her, concerned.

"Go away! You've become animals again!"

And she wept.

The dwarfs rose reluctantly and stole away into the forest, ashamed of themselves. Snow White sat a long time, a picture of distress and loneliness, but the sun appeared among the trees and she cheered up. Soon she was humming to herself.

The craving for order soon possessed me. I

appropriated a corner of the front room – the trestle bed had been knocked down – for myself. I marked off a cubicle with chalk. No one could step into that imaginary room. I kept all my school things and I often read or wrote there. Soon I knocked up a row of shelves out of discarded milk-tin boxes. All sorts of books covered them, some of which I had picked out of rubbish heaps. These were old ledgers, diaries and receipt books. The shelves looked impressive. Once I stepped over the fictitious line I couldn't be disturbed. An imperturbable insulation cut off the happenings in the other parts of the house. Sometimes my mother came rushing in, grabbed me by the shoulders and beat me.

"So you won't carry your brother for a while, ah?" she yelled.

The boy would have been bawling for some time. I jiggled him on my hips, getting him to hush quickly so I could return to my cubicle. But my hip bones bit into his plump buttocks and he cried even louder. Gradually, however, the family respected my self-imposed isolation. It was the brightest corner in the room and soon attracted admirers.

"Don't disturb him! He's reading," my mother said if any child crawled close to the lines.

I rigorously drew these demarcations, not for myself but for them. My mother didn't even dare sweep that corner – I did it myself with a salvaged wooden-handled broom. I cut out pictures from the magazines Miss Nancy left lying at the back of the classroom and pasted them on the corner walls. One I remember vividly. It was a bit of countryside sharply contrasted to the Malaysian landscape. Flowers – buttercups, I think – covered the gently undulating meadows. A boy bent down making a posy. The picture enlivened the drab plank walls and, more significantly, it fired me with a zeal for work. I could read for hours beside that picture. Another, filled with a snow-capped mountain and cloud-fluffed sky, took up the other wall.

Soon my family acknowledged that corner as my room.

"Where's the boy? I want him to deliver these clothes," Karupi, my stepmother, said.

"He's in his room," my mother said.

Karupi laughed and came to my corner.

"You can come out now. We've more important things to do," she said, smiling.

I reached Menon's house angry and paid not the slightest attention to his huge, black dog which barked furiously. Usually I stood near the cowshed adjacent to the kitchen and yelled for the cook's helper. But that day I walked boldly to the house steps beside which the brute was chained. Mrs. Menon herself came out to investigate. She scowled when she saw me.

"How many times must I tell you not to come to the house? Stay near the kitchen and call," she said angrily.

"You want to check the clothes?" I said.

She took them and disappeared into the house. I heard her stomp all over the wooden floor. The dirty linen came flying through the doorway. I picked them up and without bothering to make a bundle almost trotted home.

"Boy! You, boy! I haven't counted them!" Mrs. Menon called.

But I didn't turn around or stop. The clothes smelled in my arms like a week-old dead child. I fled from more than Menon's house. The humiliation gave me wings. I longed for the snow-capped isolation and the gentleness of the buttercupped meadows. I don't know how I reached home but it was as if Miss Nancy had led me all the way to the tidy corner with the dirt completely excluded. That night I felt, for the first time, my troubled heartbeats.

4

It was a week-end. I was bent over a book in my cubicle. The mountain poster had been replaced by a quiet but glossy view of the interior of an English house. The furniture stood as solid promises; a flower vase in the corner brightened the scene. My eyes kept turning back to the Gothic fireplace, the mantelpiece covered with gargoyle-like, tiny sculptures, the sides crammed with metallic creepers and animal heads. A black railing – the posts, glazed dwarfs – ran round the actual fireplace. A coal cauldron, polished to a shine, stood near the railing.

Karupi was talking in the other room, my father giving grunted replies.

"I tell you the boy's head is turning," she said.

"You're responsible for sending him to an English school," my father said.

"Last week he came running from Ayah's house. He didn't even let the *Amah* count the clothes," Karupi continued relentlessly.

Ayah and Amah were the honorifics for Menon and his wife. I stiffened again, recalling the humiliation. One day the Amah would respect me! Menon, who whenever he saw me crossing the field to the hospital staff quarters with a bundle of clothes, taunted me, would have to bow his head.

Amah – Honorific for Lady of high social standing.

"Not going to school, boy?" he had said.

I shook my head.

"I heard you can speak the white man's tongue better than my son," he said.

I stood, as had been dictated by the social laws of the hospital community, waiting for him to dismiss me.

"You're only good for washing other peoples' dirty clothes," he said and walked on to his house.

"He doesn't respect anybody," Karupi said.

"Maybe that's what he learns at your school," my father said.

"I'll make you talk on the other side of your face!" Karupi warned and came stomping into the front room.

"Ravi, come here!"

I looked up at her as if I saw her behind a glass panel, remote and powerless. I sat on a small rattan chair I had picked up somewhere. Karupi glared at me and advanced.

"I'll drag you out," she said.

I bent over the book.

She pulled me out but I was a coiled-up organism of legs and hands, stiff and unyielding as a tangle of metal sculpture. I felt her stinging slaps but I neither averted my face nor cried. My father pulled Karupi away.

"Don't you lay your hands on him again," he said.

I sat a long time in my cubicle, an unthinking and unreading statue. The morning changed into a bright, hot afternoon. Children's voices had silenced, adults talked in resentful tones and soon only birds twittered. The longhouse napped. I must have dozed off in the rattan chair, for suddenly everything exploded around me. The trees and fields were greener in the golden evening light. The hospital dispensary had been shuttered up for the day. Flame of the forest and bougainvillae splashed the scene. My mother gave me a mug of tea, where I sat, now on a stool beside the window.

Boys of my age crossed over from their houses to the field opposite. They kicked a football stuffed with dry grass – they couldn't afford a real one. But there weren't enough boys to even make a team of six. Ganesh got the boys under the ancient, spreading rain tree in a huddle. Even as their laughter drifted over, they ambled towards my house. During the last two months I had been put on the reserve list of most of their games. I agreed too quickly to join in their blindman's buff.

Our version was an aggressive one. The boys pushed you down and taunted you with insults. In the past the game had helped purge any ill-feeling we had for each other. I was never asked to volunteer as I hardly harboured any resentment towards them. But that evening, with malicious grins, they didn't even ask my permission. They had me blindfolded within a few seconds.

"Long time you no catch us," one of them said.

The language grated on my ear – it was the English we lapsed into after school hours.

"Long time no play," I said, reluctantly.

The day, a dim, red glow behind the blindfold, suddenly frightened me. A hostile tone had crept into the boys' voices. They dragged me away from the rain tree around which we usually played.

"Why you pull me away?" I asked in panic.

"You not man to play some other place?" Ganesh said.

The ground wobbled under my feet; this was the patch we avoided when playing football. It tripped us even when we had our eyes open.

"I play anywhere," I said.

"This body got words! See got action!" Ganesh jeered.

A jangle of animal sounds suddenly hurled itself at me. I moved first to one sound, then to another. But it was a confusing business. They kept adopting new shrieks and cacaphony. I kept moving. The calls came unexpectedly close, then shot away. Then in complete silence I was propelled through a maddening maze of twirls and whirls. I stood my ground to stop the spinning.

"Why you standing there like monkey?"

"He white monkey! No know what we think!"

"Who you call white monkey?" I shouted.

"You! You!" they chorused.

"Reading, writing more than us! You try to better teacher?" Ganesh asked.

Our termly performances had been compared. His father had given him the "puja" – our euphemism for a thorough beating – the day we brought home our report cards.

"Like girl staying in the house all time!"

"Don't touch us! Girl's hand!" they shrieked.

Blinded by rage I stumbled into the depression and fell and rose and fell. Finally I lay there not wanting to get up at all. The fury, however, awakened again and I thrashed out of the hollow in the ground. The shrilling laughter jabbed like so many knife-points that I lashed out at them.

"White monkey's hands! Keep away! Girl's hands! Don't touch!" they chanted as if they were in a classroom.

I ran at any cry, footstep, or hard breathing, with a mad man's stamina. A shirt fell into my grip and I ripped it off. The boys threw themselves at me in a free-for-all. I tore off the blindfold and swung my fists. My father came rushing out of the house on hearing the screaming and shouting.

Ganesh looked malevolently at me out of a swollen eye.

"We were just playing," he said in Tamil. "And he began tearing shirts and punching."

My father slapped me then and there. By the time I stumbled home my cheeks were flaming and swollen. My mother applied a hot, wet towel to the bruises. But I didn't cry.

"You stay home from now on! Don't join the riff-raff!" my father shouted from the front room.

"Whom are you calling riff-raff?" Govindan, Ganesh's father, called from his house.

"I'm teaching my son manners," my father said quietly.

"And how do you think I raise my family? On the white man's ideas? Soon your son will be wiping his backside with paper!" Govindan said.

"It'll be cleaner than your mouth," my father said.

"That man's calling us unclean! Where's that pariah of a boy?"

Govindan ran round the long row of houses, cornered his son and thrashed him.

Ganesh sobbed for a long time, then other sounds took over. The children cried for their evening meal. Women put pots on the fire, washed the enamel plates and mugs. Kali, the deaf attendant's short, plump wife turned the radio on full blast for the "All Indian" request programme. I slunk back to my corner and gazed a long time at the poster of the English living room. It was some time before a sort of peace returned.

School, largely coloured by Miss Nancy's presence, became the greater centre in my life. I still felt excluded from her thoughts and feelings, and her interest in dental hygiene began to wane. Our trips to the school bathrooms were part of a weekly routine. Even the men teachers, who saw us troop to the isolated, dingy building, teased us less. Miss Nancy had a serious, remote expression on her face.

Every afternoon, before lessons commenced, she opened a tin box she had on her desk. If a blue envelope peeped out of a corner she became immediately flustered, then grave, and finally inaccessible. On such days lessons moved at a painful pace. I seemed to share Miss Nancy's secret excruciation, moving about uncomfortably on my chair throughout the afternoon. The dolls, when she handled them, hung limply between her fingers. Snow White's complexion had somehow turned sickly. But Miss Nancy struggled through the stories dutifully. In the middle of narrating *Jack and Jill,* she suddenly tossed the puppets aside and picked up Humpty-Dumpty. His fall was a wreck. We were surprised at her powerful, claw-like fingers that did the destruction.

"No more fall," she announced to a bewildered class.

The afternoons were hot and clammy. We sweated through the lessons, waiting for the break. But I didn't have any respite during those twenty minutes. I shuffled about in the corridor, aimlessly. My feet always led me back to the classroom. And there sat Miss Nancy, nervously fingering a letter. Her apple, half-eaten, had been forgotten. What did she think about? If she caught me looking at her, she smiled. When lessons resumed, she became remote again and that moment of intimacy passed, unrenewed. Fearing we would be abandoned, we did anything Miss Nancy commanded.

But she was unpredictable. One afternoon she discarded normal lessons and plunged into *Hansel and Gretel.* She went on well into our hygiene hour, in fact becoming particularly excited during that narration. The landscape she set up quivered with a strange, evil energy. The model, as Miss Nancy touched it, ceased to be a plaything. The earth, though only plasticine, gave off a damp odour. The trees she used had spreading, tangling dark branches. She interwove them even further with black threads, meant to look, I think, like cobwebs. We were already frightened, merely by looking at the fragile, sooty cottage occupying a corner of the set. Then Snow White emerged as Gretel and the puppet that was often Jack or even the wolf, as Hansel.

"A long time ago," Miss Nancy began, "a little girl was lost. She was Gretel. But she had her brother, Hansel, to

look after her. They wandered a long time in a thick forest.
Their parents searched for them but in vain. The two
children were footsore and heart-weary by nightfall."

Miss Nancy's voice thickened the atmosphere, slowed
down the time, until we, like the two children, receded from
the reality of our classroom. Night was upon us and, as Miss
Nancy made the appropriate sounds, an almost touchable
fear. Miss Nancy reared up behind the cottage as a weird
apparition, chuckling deep down in her throat. A black
broom whizzed through the air and then there was only
silence. Hansel and Gretel lay on the ground, next to each
other, too tired and too innocent to worry about the dangers
that lurked around them.

The weird figure, hook-nosed and toothless, wheezed
and chuckled, hovering over the children.

"What do we have here?" crooned Miss Nancy, a
wicked gleam lighting up her eyes. "Oh, Oh! The most
delicious morsel I could hope for."

We understood "morsel" because Miss Nancy chomped
and licked her lips.

The quaintest little lamp I had seen was hung on the
dark tree beside the cottage. Miss Nancy, as the witch,
nudged the children. Startled out of their sleep, they gazed
at each other.

"I'm so frightened!" the little girl whispered, clinging to
her brother.

"Don't be afraid, Gretel, I'll find a house soon," he
said.

He craned his neck, bewitched by Miss Nancy's
fingers, in search of a light, and soon trembled with
excitement.

"I see a light!" he shouted. "I see a light!"

And some of us shouted with him, in relief.

The gloating, haunting chuckle came again.

"Now we have you," the witch said triumphantly

somewhere in the darkness. The stick loomed over the cottage roof again.

"The children, supporting each other, stepped through the night towards the points of light," Miss Nancy said.

Her face shone with the faintest drops of moisture. The eyes focused on the cottage, the lips twitched, switching from one voice to another. We marvelled at how she contained so many characters within her. As Hansel and Gretel dragged themselves to the house, Miss Nancy's excitement mounted.

In a moment which I can't ever forget, Miss Nancy transformed the cottage into a mosaic of delicious colours. The light had brightened and the children gazed, wonderstruck, at the delightful, crusty windows and walls. Hansel moved his fingers, incredulous, over the window sill.

"Chocolate!" he managed to say at last.

"Oh, I'm so hungry," the little girl said.

They fell to and they were just reaching out for the roof when the sky clashed with thunder and lightning. I think Miss Nancy had the greatest fun here. She watched our fear deepen, and, screwing up her own face let the classroom rip with the most distorted version of storm sounds we had ever heard. The children rushed into the cottage.

We didn't see any of the puppets for some time but the room filled with muffled voices. Hansel pleaded; Gretel at first whined, then cried. The witch boomed with satisfaction.

"Chomp! Chomp! Chomp! I'm going to eat your fingers, then your toes!" she chanted.

Miss Nancy's face had taken on a glazed concentration.

"Stop her! Hansel!" the girl pleaded again.

"I can't, I can't," Hansel said.

"Then your juicy calves, thighs, stomach! I'll pull out the entrails and swallow them dripping!"

Miss Nancy's face had gone shapeless. For a moment she slipped back among us and seeing the horror on our faces, relaxed into enjoyment.

"Oh, you little buggers!" she said in her own voice, affectionately.

Falling back into her play voice she uttered a terrible oath:

"I'll eat your hearts, roasted alive!"

There was pandemonium among us and within the cottage. Miss Nancy had entered an uncontrollable frenzy.

"Breasts, mouths, noses, eyes and your brains. Crack open the skull and spill the white mash!"

The Deepavali goat-slaughter flashed in my mind with vivid, viscid gore.

The children screamed and moaned but the witch's voice drowned their fear and appeals.

When I returned home that evening Miss Nancy's final expression, as she drew the puppets from inside the cottage, haunted my thoughts. A flushed, vengeful face, almost without any recognition, had been turned to us.

5

The whole of the following week Miss Nancy kept off the stories. She had reverted to her earlier correctness. Her hair was plaited and tied up with ribbons. A slim belt pinched her waist. Her blouse, laced at the neck, was a mosaic of knots. In fact, she gave off such an air of neatness she might have been a gift package. She spoke in clear, even tones and her face didn't betray the faintest blush.

She took us back to Ernie, who had grown in the interval we had abandoned him for the stories. Tom, his father, had moved the whole family to the city. He was an agricultural consultant to some firm. Ernie's mother stayed longer in bed, shuffled about slowly in the kitchen and knitted more often, waiting for her husband to come home. Ernie, lean and lanky, sporting the suit of a young man looking about himself, wandered the labyrinths of the city, attending exhibitions of farm equipment and printing machinery. He went to factories and stood sharply etched against a montage of pipes, cranes, wires, shuttling panels and bluish sparks that proliferated. We read only the simple words beneath the illustrations, but Miss Nancy conveyed the intricate pulsing hub of the British industrial network with her sometimes plastic expression, finger ballet, and fluid eye work.

Perhaps tiring from all these, Ernie took strolls in the countryside. But there was no real escape. He stood, pinned

against the thorny bushes, high-power electric cables
overhead, monstrously towering substations. When he did
get into real country, the landscape seemed a fairy-tale
creation. But this was where Miss Nancy took over and
superimposed her creations on the scene. Her fingers flitted
through the air, opening and closing like scintillating
crystals. Snow petalled down from them, piling up like a
soft cushion on the ground so that her voice seemed to
come from below, muffled and strangely rich. Or she went
into a lavish strewing of the ground with an inexhaustible
supply of flowers. But she loved snow best, and with the
most imperceptible flicker of her fingers she had it drifting
down our vision.

    Closetted with her five afternoons a week, we slipped
into this invisible country she fixed up with machinery and
bolts, snow and flowers, the trance-like glare of winter,
spring and autumn, filled with the personalities of her
stories. It was terribly exciting, a complete contrast to the
world we lived in. I longed for escape from the filthy
squabbles of my neighbours, the pettifogging playmates in
the hospital compound, and the arrogant, vengeful
administrative personnel. Returning from school was re-
entering another, primitive, time zone. The last lap, the
laterite road that led me right up to the house, was a
disappointing anti-climax. The houses, squalid, green, and
over-crowded, were unfailingly there. Some nights "White
monkey!" was hissed at me from ditches and from behind
trees.

    But the hospital compound wasn't always quarrels and
class prejudice. There was the King's birthday celebrated in
a memorable manner. Then the entrance to the gravelled
hospital road was straddled by an arch bearing the legend
"Long Live His Majesty". Lights blinked at night for a whole
week. We had seen His Majesty only in photographs and
large reproductions. That year I felt my spirit lifting, seeing

the white-bearded face at the centre of the arch. The coins I received, one at school, the other from Menon, along with other school children, didn't brighten the day so much as the visage on the arch, the national anthem and the buntings that fluttered all along the red, dusty, hospital road. Then a hand seemed to have reached out from Ernie's land and touched me in the softest depths. The week – though only two days had been declared holidays – continued to be one long festival. There was abundance everywhere. We were feted with free cinema shows, free meals and fun-fairs. There was an unmistakable benevolence in the air.

When the scaffolds came down that secure feeling fell to pieces. The buntings, unremoved because new ones would be found the following year, rotted away under the sun and rain. They became another foul outpost in my daily return to darkness and futility. After that King's birthday celebrations we went back to a puzzling but exciting Miss Nancy. She shone with determination and sense of purpose. Now a combination of mother and some other function, she nursed and pampered us. Her behaviour, I was convinced, came from an inner desperation.

The hygiene hours were resumed. Once more we trooped to the dingy bathroom, accompanied by the catcalls and taunts of the men teachers.

"What are you up to this time, Nancy?"

"Shining up the brats!" our teacher called back.

"You've to use plenty of soap," Rickie, the PE master said.

His T-shirt clung to his body; his face was pudgy and his belly pushed out. He didn't walk but danced along, and we had to jog along if we wanted to talk to him. He kept his distance from the other teachers but spoke freely with Miss Nancy. He had returned from England the year before after undergoing a specialist course. He occasionally wore his blazer, and conducted PE lessons standing under a tree. He complained of the heat.

Behind Miss Nancy's jauntiness I detected a nervousness. She bolted the door firmly once we were inside, shutting the day out. We stumbled among the sports equipment towards the long, cement tub and the pitted bathroom floor. Miss Nancy switched on the light but it was so dim we at once felt intimately thrown against each other. Some of the stiff, foreign glamour peeled from Miss Nancy's face.

She pulled up a broken-down desk and, leaning it against the far wall, spread out a white cloth. From her case she brought out a bottle of shampoo, soap, brushes and towels. These she arranged in the order in which they would be used. The presence of these articles banished the claustrophobic dinginess of the bath-cum-store room. The air had already filled with exotic perfumes from her case. We felt some new initiation would take place that afternoon, and kept away from the decorated desk.

"You don't have to be afraid. I'm not going to eat you," Miss Nancy said.

She caressed a pink towel, looking round at us. For some reason or other we shrank a little into ourselves. She gazed at Aandy, the boy who had messed up the classroom on the first day of school. That had been his outstanding performance. He had remained, from then on, a gentle, smiling presence in the class. Whenever Miss Nancy reached an exciting passage in her stories he gurgled, rolled his blue eyes and slapped his thighs. Her eyes turned on Yusuf, the perpetually bashful, round-eyed boy. Seng Seng stood in front of the boys, as he always did, hair straight as porcupine quills, stubbing his toe on the floor. Then she quickly laid her hands on one of our startled classmates.

He tugged at her hands but she, smiling, held on. His struggling body squirmed this way and that, then suddenly, as if overcome, it relaxed. Miss Nancy breathed triumphantly. She wrapped a towel round the now docile boy's neck and pinned it in place.

"Bring a chair!" she ordered.

I pushed past the boys for one.

Miss Nancy, absorbed now by a secret ritual, turned the bottles, labels front, towards her. She pulled the white cloth on the desk into a tight stretch. The brushes were arranged, following a secret configuration, near the edge. The boy who had been sitting still now turned to her with complicity. She began by anointing him with a dash of the shampoo. His hair transformed, first into a brown, thick matting, then into a globe of bubbles. Miss Nancy had reddened, and though she tried to shake them off the sweat drops rolled down her face and arms steadily. Her fingers dipped into the shampoo-clothed hair as into dough. Then she tilted his head back and rinsed his hair, her fingers stroking it gently.

"There! That's how hair ought to look," she said.

She looked at him as if she could see a bright ring of light round his head. The boy raised himself gingerly from the chair, holding himself straight.

In the weeks that followed she worked her way down. Each boy in turn acted as demonstrator for face, chest, hands, legs and feet. Miss Nancy took the various parts, cleaned them, and put them back on the different bodies, coldly and meticulously.

"What have you been shining up today, Nancy? The nose? There's a lot of snot!" Rickie, the PE master, teased on another of his returns from the field.

"The savages need cleaning everywhere," she said lightly.

The turgid-complexioned man laughed.

Miss Nancy reasoned, cajoled, jolted, mocked, "feruled" and commanded. The boys, touched, persuaded, pampered and compelled, obeyed and changed. They

certainly bristled with a new smartness. They swept their
seats, sometimes the chairs, sometimes the block of cement
near the field, before sitting down. They had given up
squatting down on the huge staircase. A few sported combs
and endlessly raked their hair. We touched each other less,
preferring to play games that involved words or mere
pointing. Whenever we listened each had a specific
mannerism: brushing back the hair, resting the chin in the
palm, placing the finger against the temple or putting our
hands in our laps. Our arms swung less, steps were more
measured. Quickly we acquired the habit of giving even the
most aimless walk a determined gait. Our skins felt taut
against the cheeks, shoulders, and back.

Ernie's life was preached at us. He had stopped
wandering among factory lots and abandoned fields.
Changed beyond recognition, he held a brief-case and
joined the multitudes in the streets. Respect and dignity was
the tight-lipped young man we saw at the bus queues. The
roads busier, the shops larger and brighter than the ones he
had been in with his aunt in Glasgow, aroused in us awe
and enchantment. In the offices he entered and left every
day we saw impressive rows of workers, each seated at a
neat, shiny desk. Ernie opened his brief-case, spread out his
papers, stacked some at his left and set to work. A bell
whirred at twelve-thirty and the office came alive. The
typists, clerks and administrators abandoned the blocks of
offices. If it was a sunny day they trooped out into the park.
Ernie, erect and self-controlled, sat among the others on the
benches eating his lunch out of a box. A passer-by greeted
him and he said something in return. He enjoyed whatever
he did: poring over charts in the office or just letting the sun
shine golden over his face and hands. As Miss Nancy read
this portion of Ernie's life her voice thickened with longing.
It quivered when it followed Ernie and his girl-friend to the
theatre, museum or restaurant.

At such moments a tormented look came into Miss Nancy's face. Her fingers could hardly turn the page over. She put the book down hastily, gave us some written work and shut herself up. I stole glances at her. When she thought we were absorbed with our assignment or were following her orders to the letter, she pulled the colourful box she had on her desk towards her. From the many blue envelopes inside, she picked one and read the note, frowning. I had once or twice seen a fairish Indian teacher slip an envelope into the box. We hardly dared to come within earshot of Mr. Veerasingham, known for his ferocity in the class he taught. He whipped an offender on his naked buttocks, a handful of rulers held fanwise. But he had a timid, anxious look whenever he came, a few minutes before the bell rang, to push in a letter and hurry away. Miss Nancy's face had reddened as she read the page; her breath heaved in her chest.

She skipped the trip to the bathroom that week. There were two more months before our first year at The English School closed. Among the Standard Ones, we, Miss Nancy's proteges, had a reputation for outdoing the others in lessons and eccentricity. Miss Nancy had put us not only in white shoes but in stockings as well. Inheriting her fussiness, we were choosy about what we ate in the canteen and about the friends we kept. Some of the Malay, Chinese and Indian teachers called us "snotty", which we took as a compliment. But some of them showed us a mild respect. Soon they ceased to be surprised at whatever we did or whatever went on in our classroom. Miss Nancy's unusual behaviour became for us the badge of elitism.

Towards the end of the year most of the books had been read. Normal lessons were covered before break; the rest of the time Miss Nancy used for narrating once more, with greater elaboration, the stories she had introduced earlier in the year. Often we supplied the voice for the

various characters, depending on our memories or
sometimes on the simple scripts Miss Nancy provided. *Little
Red Riding Hood* fascinated her so much that her final
version was a startling departure from the earlier ones.

Another letter must have been thrust into her coloured
tin box during break, for when we returned she had that
glazed, fixed look. Moving as if we didn't exist, she drew
out the plasticine landscape and toy house. The inner walls
removed, the house formed a large bedroom. Though the
side walls had been unhinged, so we could watch the
drama, the interior appeared dark and forbidding. A
perfectionist, Miss Nancy had hung thick, light-blocking
tapestries on the remaining walls. The bed, intricately
decorated, was littered with stage costumes.

Miss Nancy clapped her hands excitedly and we closed
in. She dragged out the rack on which hung the dolls. They
were a grizzled lot, having enacted so many stories
throughout the year. Snow White was ragged, Little Red
shabby and Jack aged considerably. Miss Nancy had also
placed on her desk her mending and "adaptation" kit: pieces
of cloth, needles, paints, glue, buttons and rolls of thread.
Though trembling, she worked quickly and efficiently.

She curled Snow White's tresses, rubbed red into her
cheeks, painted her lips into a rich, purple bow and stitched
on a checkered, clinging dress. The puppet had become
Snow-Red. Jack acquired a thick moustache, bushy hair and
a natty suit. Miss Nancy modified his nose so that it was
enlarged and resembled a wolf's snout. Little Red made a
plump, sensual grandma, lips roughishly turned into a smile.
With her sound panel – a collection of porcelain mugs,
lightning and thunder sheet, plastic water-dripper and a toy
xylophone – at her side, Miss Nancy looked up at us.

"In a little village in England," Miss Nancy began,
"there lived a girl named Snow-Red. She was a good girl at
times. And at times a very, very bad girl."

Miss Nancy, face crinkled with pleasure, gazed round at us to see if we were following her invention.

Aandy wouldn' t take his empty, blue eyes off her.

"When she was happy," Miss Nancy continued, "she helped her mother in the house. All the plates shone under her busy hands. There wasn't a single speck of dirt on the floor. And on the living room table stood a vase of flowers she had gathered in the fields that morning."

The xylophone chimed and we, looking at the Snow-Red puppet, superimposed on the model set of a ground lush with flowers the girl romping through them, bending down whimsically and picking a few. The sky behind her was an untroubled, rosy tint. But jarring, swirling whines came from the mugs, Miss Nancy rubbing the edges and setting them off frenziedly.

Aandy's hands went to his temples and massaged them.

"But there were dark days in her life. She sat and moped in a corner. Her mother gave her an apple and told her, 'Run off now and play, for soon childhood is done.' This only made Snow-Red cry more.

"She immediately flew into the forest nearby and, in a little round of land, did a terrible dance with such wild flinging of the hands and legs that the animals gathered behind the bushes to watch, spell-bound."

Under the clangorous jangle of the xylophone, the haunting moan of the mugs, Snow-Red trembled and twitched, head flung back, hair swimming.

Aandy gasped, slobbered; some light flashed in the deep emptiness of his eyes.

"She danced against the fading morning, the still afternoon, the silver moon and the thudding of her heart. She danced against the blood inside her! Tum-thump! Tum-thump!" went Miss Nancy.

Snow-Red, a dark form against the evening, swooned

and straightened, trod the ground and whirled into the air. Aandy had begun to slap his thigh, rhythmic and loud. Miss Nancy cast shining, grateful looks at him.

"When she returned home," Miss Nancy continued, "covered with dirt and thorns and her dress torn, her mother sent her to bed without dinner. And poor Snow-Red cried herself to sleep."

During the long pause that followed, Miss Nancy dimmed the set further by closing the classroom doors nearest the blackboard.

"There was always night in her head. Whenever she walked in the country, a good girl again, she felt eyes following her," Miss Nancy said, manipulating Jack-Wolf into a sly walk behind Snow-Red.

Sometimes he almost had his hands on Snow-Red but she turned and he slunk away. This became a game. Aandy gasped and then clapped whenever this happened. One day the pursuit-and-the-escape led to Snow-Red's grandmother's house. Only the hoarse imperious command from inside freed Snow-Red from his clutches. We laughed at this episode because the grandmother, really Little, plump Red, held her stomach as she shouted the order. Jack-Wolf turned away with a stiff, vengeful body.

"One day Snow-Red's mother sent her with a basket of food to her grandma's house. Jack-Wolf came from behind a bush.

" 'And where are you going, my pretty maid?' he said.

" 'I'm going to my grandma's,' she piped, without looking at him. Her mother had told her never to look at strangers.

" 'And why are you going there, my lovely lass?' he asked.

" 'Because she's sick and must eat!' said Snow-Red and ran off.

"Jack-Wolf had faster legs. He was at her grandma's

long before her. He pretended to be Snow-Red and called out to her grandma.

" 'The door isn't locked!' she said impatiently.

"He went in and gobbled her up in one, long, delicious moment: toes, calves, thighs, belly, breasts and face."

Grandma-Red wriggled her body in strange ecstasy, feeling Jack-Wolf's snout on her. She made no sound at all.

"When Snow-Red reached the house, it was so quiet she thought her grandma was dead. She pushed past the door and approached the bed."

Miss Nancy's voice trembled and then became taut. The manipulation of the puppets clashed and overlapped. She was totally absorbed into the drama.

"Her grandma looked different, with one shoed leg peeping out of the bed clothes. Dismayed, she placed the basket on the dresser and went nearer. Grandma wasn't sleeping. She hadn't seen such penetrating eyes before: she felt naked.

" 'What big eyes you've got, Grandma!' she said.

" 'The better to see you with, dear,' Grandma said in a voice that was more a man's or an animal's.

" 'What a great, hook of a nose you've got, Grandma!' she said, marvelling.

" 'The better to smell you out, my dear,' the voice said.

" 'What thick lips you've got, Grandma!'

" 'To kiss you a smacking one,' said the voice. "Snow-Red came close, frightened and fascinated.

" 'What muscular hands!'

" 'To hold you tight, sweet!'

" 'What fine torso, what fine thighs!'

" 'Yum, yum,' murmured the wolf-voice.

" 'What swift legs,' Snow-Red said, not quite ready to fly.

" 'The better to chase you with, buxom lass!'

"And out jumped Jack-Wolf from the bed clothes and made for Snow-Red. She ran round the room but Jack-Wolf was behind her. Panting, she said, 'No, please!' But Jack-Wolf caught up. He was on her.

" 'Not that! Not that!' screamed Snow-Red.

"But Jack-Wolf was eating her up, body and soul. And Snow-Red yelled and yelled."

We were startled ourselves. Aandy was grunting, as he would when beating a goat towards pasture. Miss Nancy had stood up, screaming, her face wet with sweat. Terrified, we watched her struggle with some demon. Aandy came to her, and our rescue. He touched her gently, knowingly, and stroked her arms. Miss Nancy was never the same from that day.

The desk, the high platform on which it stood, and the immaculate blackboard became her domain. She rarely walked among us, reverting, I think, to her former horror of contact with us. But she often looked kindly at Aandy. They had a rapport that was child-like, yet touched off a mutual respect. When another letter reached her through that coloured box, she looked up at Aandy and remained calm. The miniature landscape and the puppets were untouched.

Sometimes she made us recite poetry from a coloured, illustrated book. We went through quite a few ballads in which sons died for their families or their country or for heroism. One particular poem – I forget the title – remains deeply entrenched in my mind. It is the image of a ragged boy standing, undaunted, on the deck of a burning ship and eventually sinking with it, that refuses to die. I went, vicariously, through a refinement, the flames scorching, charring and reducing me as it did that brave, detached boy.

Miss Nancy often called on me for the reciting of this poem. I stood before the class, stiff and majestic, feeling the imagined flames roar all round me and in a cold voice uttered the words. Miss Nancy sat through the recitation, enjoying the suppression of emotion, like a statue. Aandy, during these occasions, amused himself with a monologue in a language only he understood: it was neither English nor Tamil.

"Ravi, the burning ship!" Miss Nancy called and I went to face the class.

I immersed myself in the heat of some sort of baptism. I relished the experience on such occasions for I felt I was entering a great mystery. It was also disappointing, it wasn't real enough.

Once Miss Nancy's voice rang out:

"Ernie, the burning ship!"

I faced the class automatically. Only when I was halfway through the flames I realised that I had been called by another name. Miss Nancy, oblivious to the mistake, continued to address me as Ernie. Though my classmates never called me Ernie, they didn't snigger any more whenever Miss Nancy summoned me to the front by that name.

Whether she suffered from confusion or from some wilfulness, I don't know. Perhaps she had begun to live in the world to which she had no physical access. Certainly during that period I became aware of two: the one we could create and the one to which we made daily adjustments. The latter, increasingly inflexible, at moments appeared terrifyingly foreign. My head turned more towards Miss Nancy, my heart beat expectantly at some sign she might make.

When the march to the bathroom resumed, Miss Nancy acted as a severe mother. We had to clean ourselves in the way she had demonstrated. Her revulsion for dirt drove her into maniacal, rough handling of the boys. We feared to be called out as models, slinking away to the edge of the circle round Miss Nancy. Sensing the fear, Miss Nancy returned to her gentle persuasive manner.

One Wednesday afternoon I was caught.

"Ernie!" Miss Nancy said and pulled me towards her.

I was stiff in her hands, sensing that something strange was about to happen to me. I put up a struggle but Miss Nancy was too powerful.

"A black skin shows cleanliness better," she said. "Gather round, boys!"

There was no need for such an order. My classmates were already pushing close to me seeing Miss Nancy finger my shirt buttons. Her hands trembled and her voice was hoarse. Her fingers traced lines down my chest, armpits and folds of my belly. When she touched my navel button, accidentally, the boys giggled. I trembled with embarrassment and defiance. Miss Nancy's ruthless hands went to my shorts; I tore at her but she held me against her legs.

"This fellow behaves like a big one!" Miss Nancy said, laughing.

The boys laughed loudly either from relief or at watching someone else's hot shame. I was imprisoned against Miss Nancy's skirt and she pulled down my shorts gently but firmly.

"There, there," she said, calming me down.

I was still for a moment in the flesh of her arms for I smelled a familiar, comforting presence. But my buttocks contracted convulsively as she turned me around, touching my body with gentle remonstrance.

"Here, here and here," she said, talking more to herself than to the boys.

"The worst dirt spot," she pronounced with solemn relief.

Her last touch was just beneath my scrotum.

The boys clamoured round me, pressing their fingers all over my body when Miss Nancy threw me into the water.

"In he goes!"

The boys cheered. I struggled, bobbing up against the

grasping cold. But Miss Nancy fished me out again, to soap my body over, scrub it with a sponge and chuck me back into the water. I don't know whether her ritual love for cleanliness or the end of the ordeal gave me a light-headed feeling. I enjoyed the final luxury of her large, enveloping towel. It was like entering a foreign, luxuriant land. I had been immersed!

"Ernie! Ernie! Ernie!" the boys chanted.

Miss Nancy smiled at them, her face glistening with sweat from her exertions.

Though she allowed me more often near her, she was withdrawn the rest of the year. I hung around her desk while she ate from a plastic box during recess. I felt her loneliness beneath all her bustle and efficiency. I had crossed the colour bar and entered the snow country of her imagination.

At the end of the year she married an English army officer. Her husband, a tall, tough-looking man with a brush moustache, blinked at us, rocking on his heels. Miss Nancy looked far away in a new dress with long, lace sleeves. I stepped forward with our present of a tray and tea set, with the words, "Hope you'll enjoy snowy England, Miss Nancy." There was no grip in the slight handshake she offered.

6

My early experiences of life, if I say it only now, were frustratingly fragmented. There was no direction or pattern. My life has been a ride on a roller-coaster: I come into a breath-taking view of the horizon and then down I plunge. I was never allowed to get comfortable. I swirled through events or expectantly waited for them. In the end I learned to enjoy the moments as they came.

The roller-coaster glimpse of Miss Nancy's world remained as a throbbing numbness all over my body and mind that first school holidays after my first year at school. I don't know what I mourned, but there was a reaching down into an inner silence. My face, shut-up and expressionless, hovered among others' and the daily chores as a face that couldn't adjust to grief. But living in the past was only a temporary relapse. The people around me didn't linger too long over happenings now inaccessible and remote. Influenced by this attitude and only vaguely aware of a sense of loss, I was reabsorbed into the pulse and rhythm of the long-house activities.

Watching from the cell of uncertainty, I let the harsh and only rarely smooth cadences of life in that row lead me. We had even learned to enjoy boredom, a luxury of flow among the patternless, distracting events. Days appear as arrested moments. There is the afternoon when the houses are silent. Men and women, depending on who dominates the household, lie in the doorways, supple and eager for the thinnest breeze. Children are sprawled on the verandah cement, abandoned to rest. A couple of dogs drowse at their feet, fleas a voluptuous cloud over them. In the still air, the nude children's bodies, the women's blouses, the green house pillars, the spreading trees and the hospital surgery and offices are sharply etched against an innocent, blue sky.

Then the afternoon stirs like a rustle of paper. Over the sleeping bodies a couple of women stand, conspiratorial, in the doorways, weaving strange signs with their hands. A tap squeakingly turned on in the communal bathroom gashes the silence explodingly. Water pours down a body and thuds on the floor. The single cotton tree, two houses away from mine, crackles, and a pod splits down the middle, the black seeds raining to the dry ground. A child bawls himself, lustily, out of a dreamless sleep. A woman hushing him sings an invigorating lullaby, more to awaken than to soothe back into slumber.

Long shadows appear on the grass beyond the houses. The sun has shifted, the mood has changed. Windows open in the surgery and a bunsen burner hissingly cuts the stillness. Attendants return from their morning shift; women already in the houses stumble to the cooking places and poke the ashes for a smouldering ember to start the fire for tea.

In a few minutes there is no sign of the sleep that covered most of our bodies and minds. The afternoon, roasted, has now turned pleasantly fragrant. Strange perfumes – blood fixed on slides, urine boiled over white flames, potassium permanganate-stained breezes – drift towards our houses. Voices are already loud over the glass and metal tinker in the laboratory opposite the houses.

Out on the warm, evening field children make desultory attempts at play. Girls run round the huge rain tree, giggling, flouncing, and then slump against the rough trunk. This is the prelude to more organised games. Boys lunge at each other with mysterious viciousness, pulling down imagined enemies by the hair. I never could decide whether the cries of pain were real or simulated. This haphazard, robust spilling of energy went on until Ganesh and Azmi, the midwife's son, appeared on the scene. They tapped an unbouncing, grass-stuffed football between them, dressed in the mockery of professionals. Ganesh had on the strangest assortment of stockings, garters, shorts and T-shirt. Azmi wore resplendent white which his mother washed every day and beat him for dirtying.

Brutality, when finally two teams had been formed, characterised the game. Ganesh acted as referee and star-player and shouted, hustled and intimidated everyone into the rough discordance of the game.

"No kick the ball on Ayah's cowshed!" he warned at the beginning of the game. "I cave in your teeth."

"Clothes line here boundary," Azmi said, gesturing towards the wires strung between the young angsana trees.

These forbidden areas could make or mar any game. Once a ball or stick crossed these lines it was impounded. Amah, Menon's wife, had a hawk's eye for such straying missiles, and had the gardener pounce on them. In the middle of an exciting match when we forgot everything else, our frenzy running high with the rhythm of the game, the ball flew over and we watched, sagging, the man grab it. We would sit around on the field, pathetically accusing each other, then throw appealing glances at the large bungalow. We only heard the children's laughter there and Amah's raised voice. The following day one of our fathers, pleading almost on bended knee, would retrieve the ball.

On casualty-free days our shouts ticked through to nightfall as if we were grasshoppers who hated to see the day die. Night fell inevitably. The laterite approach to the "lines" gloomed over. The guava trees at the bend shrouded themselves in mist; the old bungalow, rarely used and only by Englishmen, became exotically distant. From the field, where we still played, the row of houses (the "lines"), appeared as a primitive collection of dim, furzy-edged spawning light. You heard the gruff voices, the tinkling kitchenware, the harsh putting down of babies into sleep. Then, to break this seeping, domestic peace, came Ratnam's shrill, cursing voice up the crunching, gravelled track.

What began as a faint muttering reached obscenity-textured desperation as he neared the mango tree beside Sulaiman's house. They were neighbours, but Ratnam's unquiet tongue allowed only a victim-suppressor relationship. Sulaiman, Menon's right-hand man, had to keep the labourers in order. Ratnam too often shattered his ego-dominated authority. But Ratnam hadn't always been a careless, babbling rebel. He had been, I remember, an upright, quiet man who prized cleanliness above everything else. It was reassuring to see him bent over the foul-smelling drains every morning. He heaped the balls of paper, bottle lids, crushed cardboard cartons, with which we clogged up the drains, on the grass verge, leaving them there like accusing fingers.

"We smell as foul inside as this drain," he said in irritation.

Sometimes he wielded the broomstick like a lash and made the boys remove the rubbish from the drains. At the end of the day, after work, he scrubbed his body scrupulously clean and sat at a yellowing book on a stand, though he didn't know how to read. He turned the pages, most of them filled with illustrations, chanting. His wife, fair, bangled, perpetually covered by a sari, gave him rice-water in a silver vessel. But one evening he came back to a wife writhing on the floor, her mouth foaming. A few months after her death he fought with Muthiah, the hospital dispenser, and beat him up badly. He was tried and convicted. He left his work to his young son, to serve a five-year prison sentence. When he returned he was a changed man. In a dramatic gesture he burnt the ancient book and took to the bottle. His mania for cleanliness intensified. Though you smelt *samsu* on his breath even during the mornings, he wielded the brush as a scourging whip. It might have been the work, or his feelings; by evening he had all but collapsed.

Then he went to town and returned to enact the drama, we, the children, eagerly awaited.

"Mother-foulers! What are you staring at?" he cursed when he saw us.

He stumbled up the dark-red, laterite road.

Our mothers called to us, but we were not to be coaxed or threatened. Something in the man held us spellbound.

"That man and his tongue!" a woman wailed hopelessly.

"My tongue licks only my own saliva," Ratnam said quietly, following an esoteric logic. "It doesn't stray, tell lies or foul other peoples' lives."

We had trailed him to Sulaiman's house. The man himself stood behind the wooden railings – his was a more enclosed house – looking sternly at the group.

"Ratnam," he said, "go quickly to bed. The Ayah is angry with you."

"Who's Ayah? Has he a white backside?" Ratnam said.

"You should know. You're the one who washes the toilets," Sulaiman said sharply. "Now go!"

"You think you can order me about?" Ratnam said and spat at the mango tree. "Can you stand in the toilets, in other peoples' stink as I do, for one hour?"

---

samsu – Illegal alcoholic brew.

"That's why you've a dirty tongue?"

"But a clean heart, a clean heart!" Ratnam said, slapping his breast. .

He had found a wife for his son from one of the neighbouring estates. Most evenings, after he returned primed with toddy and samsu, he abused her soundly.

"Have you been dragging your backside all over the floor? It smells too clean! You women are all the same. Clean outside, dark inside!" he shouted.

The daughter-in-law's elder child wailed. She carried the younger, a girl, on her hip.

"Hold the boy for a while," she told the man, ignoring his foul remarks.

"Don't bring him near me! Your son may not be my grandson," he said.

Almost as a kind of bribe, the aging man took out a pungent, oily package. He thrust it at the boy – vadais he had probably bought from my grandmother, Periathai. At another time he produced a rattler. The shiny bicycle he had bought for the boy now leaned against the wall, one of the wheels gone, the paint erupting like boils and flaking off. Ratnam somehow found the money to keep his daughter-in-law in jewelry. That particular evening a quarrel raged around this young woman's gold.

Muniandy had scolded her only that afternoon for sporting the thick necklace and and the heavy bangles.

"Why show the world everything you have?"

"You didn't make them for me," she said.

"Are you wearing them to spite me? I can already see the neighbours looking at me in a funny way," he said.

"Let them be jealous. Gold is for wearing," the young wife said.

"They will slash your neck for it," Muniandy said and went back to work.

Women and young girls had gathered round

Muniandy's wife in the communal bathroom. We heard the praise gather like a storm cloud over us. By that time I had learned that if a person or thing was held up for adulation, deeper, more destructive events followed. Even my mother, who dressed sloppily and had little say in the acquisition of household wealth, came back from the gathering muttering to herself.

"That goldsmith sweated for days over that jewelry. Cutting his own throat has turned his head," she said. "My wedding jewelry shines with a poor light."

Pather – the Tamil word for goldsmith – was a legend among us. He had come round to the houses, when he began setting up shop, to woo clients. My mother used to listen to his talk as he hammered out ear-rings, nose-rings, toe-rings; cut, through words, into the exquisite gold of the woman's imagination. The houses rang with his "golden" tales for hours, and a few families ended up debtors to him. Patiently, and at every payday, he visited us to collect what little we could spare. When the debts had been settled, he ceased to come. But the women always went to him. An afternoon trip to Pather became the thing – it added the gloss to otherwise lacklustre lives.

Then one morning Pather was found in the back cubicle of his long, narrow shop, moaning, and his neck – where he had made the slash with a barber's blade – thick with blood. They didn't understand his mutterings, mingled as they were with the air hissing through the barely severed throat. Much of the vivacity was gone when he returned from the hospital, but his eyes had a penetrating, steady focus. He never looked people in their faces, only at their hands.

"How we visited him in hospital!" my mother said. "Look at him now! Making fine jewelry for a drain-sweeper's daughter-in-law!"

If you produced the money he produced the

excellence. Anyone who went to him had to be well-off, if not wealthy. Prosperity and status were revealed in oblique ways. Language was inadequate. Young as I was, I recognised that words were merely a medium; that they externalised a tiny fraction of what we felt. In our community they formed only the surface. The speech, often staccato, coarse, unending and seemingly unnecessary, sounded rich. They came from an imagination that had withered because that clutter I was later to identify as culture wasn't there. The subtle, blending nuances having been removed, words became knife-thrusts. Yet they were hopelessly outside ourselves. Imagination had been replaced by fractious feeling; I wasn't comfortable in all the talk that stormed over my head.

I depended more on the discordant – if this is possible – rhythm that lay behind the words and moved the people to action. It led a series of swirling, destruction-edged, waters to the eye of the evil whirlpool. Then the stasis was the contentment that comes from the knowledge that everything you hated had been removed completely. My desire and theirs had a similar pattern but the ends were different: building through stages I hoped to hold on to something, they to nothing. So everything was used, even Ratnam.

"O, the great *Jamindar* has come back!" Letchumi, Govindan's wife, said loudly from three houses away. "He thinks he owns everything."

"He certainly has you within his hands," Govindan said.

"I'm not like his daughter-in-law. Nobody has me," Letchumi said.

This family discussion was an extension of the Ratnam drama – they baited him. His daughter-in-law, Anjalai,

---

Jamindar – Land-owner, used in Malaysia with deprecatory edge.

busied herself, turning a deaf ear to the dark insinuations.
But Ratnam, sensitive to such barbs, shouted back retorts.

"You're everybody's daughter-in-law!"

"Don't open your shit-stinking mouth, Ratnam!"
Govindan warned. "I'll push a broomstick down your throat."

"The cashier is speaking to me? How was the showing
today? Did many men buy your wife's wares?" Ratnam said.

"Do you think I'm Anjalai? Do you think that thing she
wears round her neck doesn't come from men wearing
themselves around her?" Letchumi yelled.

"Who are you calling a prostitute?" Anjalai, roused,
screamed back.

"I didn't say that at all," Letchumi said sweetly. "Only,
you go around showing your neck, arms and whatever else."

We didn't know what the words meant but we caught
the savagery behind them. I was revolted. Events speeded
up. Govindan thumped the wall every time he slung an
oath, for emphasis. Letchumi set up a whining, indignant
wail. Ratnam hunted the house wildly for some weapon.
Anjalai cried in between retching up coarse invectives. The
children stood at a distance, watching, listening.

"You painted, tarnished flesh! Leave my Anjalai alone,"
Ratnam said.

"She's not yours. Your son's. May be your toddy-
blindness stops you from seeing," Letchumi called back.

"See what filth she's throwing at us, *Mamah*," Anjalai
wailed.

"I can go to prison again! Where's that iron rod?"
Ratnam bellowed.

Muniandy walked into the quarrel at that moment.

"You've been displaying your jewelry! The evil snakes
are hissing again," he said and thrashed his wife.

"Don't touch the girl!" Ratnam said.

Mamah – Father-in-law.

"She's my wife!" Muniandy yelled.

"Who says? Not the urine-drinking old drain scrounger!" Govindan said.

Muniandy, enraged, ran round to Govindan's house.

"Come out if you've a muscular tongue!"

"The scented, painted thighs!" Ratnam yelled.

"Like father, like son!" Govindan jibed.

"Stop all this noise!" Sulaiman called, but he went unheeded.

The men had scrambled to the grass patch in front of their houses and stood slinging words like Indian fighting sticks. Ratnam, wobbling from his drunkenness and emotion, flung himself at Govindan.

"Leave him to me!" Muniandy said and thrust his father away.

Muniandy and Govindan thrashed on the ground, arms, legs and curses, when we heard the crunch on the gravel. We, the children, fled immediately and watched from windows and doorways. But Muniandy, Govindan and Ratnam, lost in their hatred, went on struggling, locked among themselves. A shining, club-like stick landed on their bodies. The men fought even more desperately. Then silence.

Ayah stood above them.

He separated them, stood them up individually and once more the club flashed. The men grunted.

"Don't beat my husband, Ayah," Letchumi pleaded.

"Your husband, ah?"

A renewed fall of the club. Govindan slumped to the ground.

"No stick on you. Vermin!" Ayah said.

He kicked Ratnam down, his boots landing again and again on soured, fragile bones.

The boots crunched away. No one spoke. The night was a long wait for morning. And the next day we moved about, all of us, as if we had offended God.

Ayah or Menon was rarely seen, except on official business. He had acquired some special, curative touch from watching the visiting – twice a week – doctor at work. We saw a humble, efficient Menon when the white man descended from his chauffeur-driven car. Then he hung around the man, issuing orders in Tamil or coming down to our level by cursing in dialect. Once the car rounded the bend, the red dust partially hiding it from view, Menon reassumed his stature as Ayah. With that returned English and its, even if coloured by South Indian twists, accents.

Sometimes, during the school holidays, we gathered at the surgery entrance, the morning sun warming our skins. A groaning woman with a protuberant belly would be guided up the steps to wait for Ayah. Or a young labourer who had got into a fight over a straying wife, brow opened up, was rushed in. The shirt, soaked red, and the incoherent mumbling fascinated us. Or an old man sat on the wooden bench beside the steps, wrinkled, stupid with age and intolerably in pain. These created a real, challenging world. Many of us sighed, knowing we could never even dream of becoming doctors; that would be "biting the hand that fed us", namely, the benevolent Ayah.

Led by Ganesh, we fashioned stethoscopes out of string and bottle lids; the filament, glass stem in a discarded bulb, was the thermometer. Ganesh was Ayah, Azmi the visiting M.O. and I played Govindan, the attendant in the surgery. We added a satirical edge to the game solely to prove to ourselves how inaccessible were the real roles. The smaller boys lined up as patients, some of them impersonating women.

Ganesh tap-tapped a 'pregnant' woman.

"Your stomach is big. Have you got a baby cow there?" he said.

"Ayah will deliver me from such a problem," the

'woman' said.

"Govindan, take the temperature!"

I did so. Ganesh scrutinised the glass tube.

"Nothing to be afraid of. Your time isn't near," he said.

The 'woman' walked laboriously away only to set up a blood-curdling wail at a yard. Then everyone rushed about in an 'emergency'. The 'woman' was carried back on an improvised stretcher.

Ganesh, trembling, wiped his forehead. He meddled about with the 'woman's' legs, then looked at me.

"Call the M.O.?"

He nodded solemnly, defeated.

One of the small boys "vroomed" in. Azmi, dignified and holding a more sophisticated stethoscope, alighted.

"What's the matter, Menon?"

"Difficult case."

The 'M.O.' examined the patient. Then stood in his classical pose, stethoscope awry, hand cupping an elbow (the patient mockingly moaning), contemplative.

"We've a caesarian on our hands, Mr. Menon. Operation," the 'M.O.' said.

"Disrespectful, wicked boys!" Ratnam, sober and responsible, was upon us. "Making fun of big men."

Somehow word travelled to Ayah's bungalow. We were hauled up; the dog barking beneath the stairs, we were given whacks on our bottoms with a *rotan*.

We were summoned for doing and for not doing. I remember my anxiety to speak English again, to revive Miss Nancy's world, during that bleak holiday period. The language we spoke in the long verandah of the houses was a defiant version of English, mingled with and sounding very Tamil. The minute we broke into "pure" English we were scolded.

---

rotan – Cane.

"You'll have Ayah's anger on our heads!"

But English, as spoken by teachers in schools, reigned supreme among the more skilled, educated personnel of this estate hospital. They lived, quite removed from us, on raised terrace houses. The walls, brushed over with better quality yellow paint, the cream-and-red *chicks* and the row of toilets with a common flushing system, distinguished them from us. The contacts between us were functional and brief. An attendant was allowed to tap on the back door for the midwife in an emergency. Very rarely, a boy from the "lines" ran to summon Kai Pang, the clerk, because the M.O. was making an unscheduled inspection.

Visits on a social level were taboo and discouraged. Violation meant, for the children, two beatings: one from our parents, the other from Ayah himself. The adults had to forfeit their visits to town. Men, particularly, resented this: they couldn't down their daily pint of toddy. The women attendants were carefully inspected at returning-home time. They were usually allowed to take back "something" from the hospital kitchen, but not when they had offended.

Only very few people from the "lines" were privileged enough to make social visits to the "yellow territory". They accepted, though rarely stated, their status as pariahs, that is, parasites. Their bearing, proud in our midst, was suitably honed down to a humble, waist-bending, eyes-averted posture the moment they passed the angsana trees, the border between the "lines" and the yellow houses. The back door was opened to them; they squatted on the kitchen floor, waiting for the family to finish its meal and hand the left-overs to them. One woman attendant, Mariamah, gray-haired and the unacclaimed rich woman in the "lines", accepted such prescribed social rules and went bending her knees for her daily meals.

---

chicks – Bamboo wickerwork used as sunshade.

The others could cross the no-man's-land, the playing field, only on festival days: Chinese New Year, Deepavali or Christmas. On such occasions, more out of curiosity than the need to beg, many of us put on penitent, impoverished airs and stole towards the staff quarters. Among the aloof, status-conscious families, was one which celebrated the Christian spirit: charity towards all, evil towards none. Mrs. Xavier, midwife, separated from her husband, had that exotic thing that characterised Christmas for me for many years to come: bon-bons. She cajoled, persuaded and even forced us to pull them with her children, to be rewarded by a glassbead-like sweet and that legend of our fortunes on a bit of paper.

I smuggled myself one dusk, when the "lines" children raged on the field in their wild games, the men either drunk or getting drunk, the women gossiping in several doorways, a time, in fact, of shadow and secrecy and individual preoccupation, towards the staff quarters. I hid in the bushes beside the last house, the one that could be seen from Ayah's bungalow, but well-concealed, and looked on. Boys wheeled about on their bicycles. Women stood over prams, talking. A car, a Hillman Minx, was parked in front of one of the houses. I watched, like an alien shuttled in from a primitive world. The clean clothes and the casual, free air about them astounded me. The scene awoke strange desires. One boy, plump, and apparently on some mischievous fling, came by, sniffing.

"Don't you hide there, Mike!" a girl called. "There are creatures there that crawl!"

"I'll put a worm down your back!" the boy said cheerfully.

"Mummy! Mummy! Mike's being wicked again!"

The boy saw me before I could get away.

"What are you doing here?" he said sternly, though not unkindly.

"Watching."

For a moment he stood speechless, eyeing me as he would a snail that had slithered into a well-tended flower bed. Then he smiled.

"I know you, Ravi. I'm Mike," he said and extended, as if he had been tutored to do so, his hand.

I grasped it briefly and then began to slide out of the bushes.

"Come again!" he called and I mistook his invitation for practised politeness.

But somehow word had got home that I had been "there". I did hear a tread and a mumble while I had been hiding. Mariamah may have carried the news. The effect was strange and upsetting.

The family was collected in the back room, nearer the cooking place. Neighbours looked at me in a preoccupied way, deliberately plunging into a simulated conversation with whoever was within earshot. As I entered the front room, my mother noted my arrival coldly. She hurried to the clamour in the other room; my sisters and brothers had persuaded her to repeat one of her simple stories. They quietened down when she resumed the tale. Their clapping marked their enthusiasm. I ambled in. My mother went on; the boys and girls ranged round her hardly bothered to lift their heads. At the fireplace, Karupi who had seen me come into the room, abruptly changed the subject, talking with her neighbours. Usually she made a nasty remark on my late appearance.

The silent boycott continued into the next morning and evening. Even the boys refused to play with me. At dusk my father called me.

"Ayah wants to see you," he said without looking at me, so acknowledging I had committed a grave crime.

Bewildered and frightened I set out for the bungalow, knowing what awaited me. The black dog greeted me with stomach-turning growls. Amah saw me, tossed her head a little and went on arranging flowers on a table. I stood, as I had never been allowed to, near the staircase so that the censure could be effective and complete. The cook sat outside the kitchen munching sireh without a glance in my direction. He always had a smile for me when I went with the bundle of washed and ironed clothes.

A newspaper rustled to the floor. I knew the Ayah's appearance would be dramatic, the children had stopped their chatter or thumping runs on the plank floor. Ayah cleared his throat and the wooden floor shook a little. Suddenly he was leaning over the balustrade. He held the rotan in his right, stronger, hand.

He stomped down the steps, halted within hand's reach of me and struck first at my shoulders, then at my legs. I wanted to cry, not so much at the pain but at the incomprehensibility. He said not a word. The silence infuriated me.

As I stumbled back, weak with disgust and confusion, I felt all the old nausea return. The field I crossed wasn't covered with grass but with the vomit of thoughtless living; it was the slave patch on which one was driven relentlessly, cornered and whipped. Over it rose a sky dark with cruelty, injustice and irrationality.

I don't know what promises I made myself but a grain of iron must have entered my soul for, from the following day, I turned away from the God who ruled my people.

7

When I reached my fifth year in The English School, I suddenly noticed that it had changed since Miss Nancy's time. A covered walk connected the main building and the two annexes at both its wings. The field had been widened; a small, wooden building put up for Nature Study. The canteen had expanded so that the original counter and room served the staff; the extension, open on three sides, catered for the boys. The library, still located in the hall, had a partitioned reading room; the shelves had increased, more new books in circulation. I read widely: Biggles on his many wartime missions, adventures of the Famous Five, Sherlock Holmes, and, occasionally, abridged versions of Dickens or Shakespeare. I stayed back after school, at least once a week, to read in the library. Or I joined the seniors in the fortnightly screening of the Cinema Club. One film I can never forget is *Odd Man Out* for it stirred me strangely.

The English School had stopped taking in students for Standard One. A separate school had been built for the lower classes, across the main field. My school was soon to be only a secondary school. Old teaching methods had slowly been discarded. It was rare to hear of pupils being caned in the class or made to memorise pages for not handing in homework. Rumours of a government examination to be introduced the following year filled us with fear. Altogether schooling was not the haphazard business it had been. I took pride, perhaps responding to the efficiency the school exuded, in going to my lessons every day. I had Chinese and Malay friends, but we rarely met outside school and then only briefly.

That year too, I noticed a change in my father. Unlike the other men in the long-house, who went to Sungai Petani for Tamil films and samsu, he remained at home. He was either in the laundry or at the ironing table. When he did go into Bedong, he would chat with his goldsmith or barber friends. That year he looked collapsed. Growing absent-minded, he sat at the table out on the verandah. The black cigar he was fond of would have gone out. A few lines had appeared on his face and he rarely smiled.

"I want some money to buy a book," I said one evening.

"You think money grows on trees?" he growled.

One morning he slapped my mother when she asked for marketing money. Karupi kept out of his way. Then men appeared at the house on pay day.

"Got a drink for me today?" *Bayi* said.

He wore a khaki shirt and shorts, patched in one or two places, but he arrived punctually at the hospital office where Kai Pang doled out the pay packets. Vadai-vendors, the ice-cream and candy-floss men, waited as patiently on those still, hot, exciting afternoons. The children were on their best behaviour. When their fathers came down the office steps, they ran to them, to hug and to point.

But shop-keepers and money-lenders grabbed them even faster.

"What fathers and mothers are these? Nothing for their children?" the vadai-seller remarked loudly.

---

bayi – Slang reference to North Indian.

That was the last we saw of him.

"No beer. Take what money I can give and go," my father said impatiently.

"Never mind the money, Kannan. Ask the boy to get some beer," Bayi said.

"And next month the debt will be a tight knot round my neck!" my father said.

The turbanned Bayi clucked and drank the tea my mother had prepared. Long after Bayi had gone, my father sat immobile against the specious, fragile mirth all around him, of pay day. His black cigar gleamed like an extra cat's eye in the gathering darkness.

On Saturdays I cycled to the Big House. This was the first bungalow-mansion in Bedong and the man who built it, Pillai, a few years before awarded the JP, lay recovering from or seized by some illness, alone in his large room. Downstairs – I passed the walls going up to fetch the dirty linen – was ranged a pictorial history of the man. He had risen from a complacent-looking, hair-parted young man in a dark suit to the gun-shouldering hunter-companion of some Englishman. The most magnificently framed photograph showed the aging, urbane Pillai serving tea to foreign visitors.

The gates to this house were at least ten yards from the porch. Black Alsatians growled, flexing their limbs menacingly at my approach. I held my breath and trundling the rickety bicycle noiselessly as I sneaked to the back courtyard and kitchen. Even if the dogs attacked I couldn't be saved. Pillai's son and his family, the other occupants of the house, were too far away, living where the servants' quarters would have been in a colonial bungalow.

I parked the bicycle on the cement courtyard and waited for the rush of water from the drain pipes. I always wondered why the old lady, Pillai's wife, made a ritual of her bath on Saturdays. Then the water rush ceased.

"Boy! Come up with the clothes!" I heard.

I ascended the dark staircase to the musky, even gloomier room. Life seemed to have stultified in this room. Only a portion of the large bed was used, the sheets stained with the fluids of senility and imminent death. But the old lady, a pair of vulture eyes mounted on a stick, followed every one of my movements. If, after I had bundled up the wet linen, I stood significantly over it, the eyes immediately turned away.

"Why are you standing there?" the old woman croaked at last.

I stood, head down, eyes on the floor.

"Beggars!" she shouted and a balled note fell at my feet.

Back home I played the empty-handed, turned-away mendicant.

"Nothing?" Karupi said, looking at my face.

I shook my head. Then when she was about to slide away, disappointed, I placed the five or ten-dollar bill, still crumpled, in her palm.

"You could have smoothed it out," Karupi remarked.

"I'm not going again," I said.

"We'll see," Karupi said.

One night, when we had gone to bed late – the dinner had been late, my grandmother returning with the money after dark – I heard the walls being thumped, bodies shuddering against the planks, the rotan land with a sickening thud on sleep-chocked flesh, moans.

"O, you laze-abouts! I break my bones filling the rice pots every day!" my father cried.

"We aren't used to tapping," Karupi protested, groaning.

My mother was crying.

"Kill and bury me! I didn't ask for children!" she screamed hysterically.

The rotan fell repeatedly, ruthlessly.

In the morning the house rang with the children's clamour for food. My grandmother and I fed them tea and old biscuits. My mother, Karupi and Father had left the house very early.

"Gone to tap in Riverside Estate," my grandmother said.

So began the nightmare existence of my family. The two women returned at about two, my father having come back to the laundry around ten, covered with latex smell, their shoes webbed with white, dried rubber strands. The food tasted bland; there were no stories at night.

I had to report to the laundry in the afternoons, after a hurried meal, when I returned from school. My grandmother sorted the clothes I plucked off the twined-rope clothes line. The chore became mechanical, my eyes dazzled by the hypnotic glare of the white, dried clothes. I only heard my heart-beats, the regular toned-down breathing. Then it was enough to see the piles of clothes sorted out and tied into bundles for the ironing table. The eyes looked out of perpetual fatigue, the mind swallowed by the whiteness.

The house was in continual uproar; the struggles even among the young became brutal. Watching my infant brothers and sisters, I only felt disgust. Their eyes were trained on nothing but the bottle or bowl, their ears caught the tinkle of glass and their mouths chanted food or chewed, their hands grasped the ball of rice or the occasional banana. Or they swiped at the face across the plate.

Karupi and Mariamah, the woman attendant, still gossiped in the evenings. My stepmother had grown defiant again: she often feigned fatigue and, gorged on the food Mariamah salvaged from the hospital quarters, slept long before any of us did.

But Bayi continued to show up at our house on pay

days. My father capitulated and sent me out for the large
Stout the man drank quickly, all by himself.

Some afternoons I stayed back even longer at school.
It was a relief to read the adventures of English schoolboys.
When my two mothers had been going to Riverside Estate
for about a month, I was almost every day in the library. I
read like the parched, desperately postponing the return
home.

The house looked empty when I got there. The
children lay sprawled on the trestle bed in the back room,
their bodies covered with filth. My imaginary room would
have been invaded, the "filler" books strewed about on the
floor. My mother slept in an isolated corner, huddled. My
father, a dim figure in the laundry, still swung clothes over
his head. My grandmother sat on the darkening grass,
folding and bundling clothes. Karupi could be heard
laughing with Mariamah. In the other houses radios blared
the evening Tamil request songs. Ratnam had come back
from the toddy shop and curses rose above the other noise.

"When will this man pull out his filthy tongue?"
Letchumi said for all to hear.

"When his hands wither. They will too. Anjalai sucks
his blood for gold," Kali, Chevudon's wife, consoled aloud.

"Where's the food you cooked this afternoon? Why do
I have to eat bread soaked in tea every day?" Chevudon said
above his deafness.

From the field came the children's roar at play.

Sulaiman, in his house, recited the Koran.

One of my sisters came back from the other houses,
howling. My mother leapt up, seized the girl and beat her.

"Why do you wander around like an orphan? Is it for
this we get through mist and sun every day?"

My sister screamed, cried and kicked her legs on the
floor.

"What's that boy, the eldest, doing? Where has he been

the whole day?" my mother shouted in sudden rage.

"Eating pig flesh!" Karupi called from Mariamah's house.

"He'll eat cow flesh," my mother said.

I sat in my ruined cubicle, blind and deaf to everything. When I had slumped, hungry, into an uneven sleep, I was pulled up and thrashed. My father stood over me a long time, watching me whimper.

"I won't deliver clothes any more! The Big House can wait and wait!" I mumbled, between sobs.

"We'll see," Karupi, who had returned to see me beaten, said. "You're showing your tail too much."

My father slapped her and pushed her away.

"You're no better, you loin-cloth wearer!" she shouted, stumbling away.

But my father caught her again and the rotan choked the curses in her throat. All around, the children wailed. My sister, a year younger than I, went into an uncontrollable spasm on the floor. My mother rushed to her. After a while, Karupi joined her and they applied lotions.

The house fell silent; my father resumed his statue pose at the table outside.

With the sums I saved up I bought comics. Thursdays were important, liberating days. The fresh smell of foreign, unthumbed pages and the bright colours lifted my spirits. *Beano, Dandy* and *Topper* nestled in my schoolbag like gold parchment after I had stopped at the Nalla Book Store on the way to the bus-stand. I never read them immediately; the bus was noisy, the petrol fumes nauseating. I didn't want to waste absorbing adventures, pranks and fantasies against such distractions. My cubicle and my home were needed for the self-surrender. At home I gobbled down my lunch and retired to my corner of the front room. I didn't mind the pestilent, unceasing bawling of the children. Soon I didn't hear anything.

"Desperate Dan" and "Lord Snooty", recognizable characters, absorbed me the most. Dan took me through hilarious, liberating episodes. The huge cow-pie he swallowed, his tough head and saw-toothed bristles formed part of a raucous escape from my surroundings. Then, when I had had enough of twisted lamp-posts, tilted roofs, overturned double-decker buses, I slid into the graceful, anaemic but ordered world of Lord Snooty. The quiet schemes, the faithful companionship and a benevolent aunt calmed and invigorated me. *Topper* rounded off the evening with an uninhibited surrender to facile pranks and jokes. During the week-end I went through them several times.

These comic strips had a strange but pleasant effect on me. I felt, for instance, I could face anything. They turned everything I knew into an unrecognizable adventure. On the days I read them, my work in the laundry – I reported late and remained only for a while – moved fast. Karupi could taunt and insult me but I only smiled or easily switched my mind off. Karupi glided away, infuriated. The curses and oaths around me, issuing from several houses, lost their vulgarity. Ratnam seemed such a poor joke of a man; the Ayah a robot, easily short-circuited, of power.

With no adults in the house during the morning, Ragini, Karupi's sister, only fifteen, my brothers and sisters, wandered all over the long-house for playmates and food. When I returned from school, Ragini, full of complaints, placed the plates and dishes on the table roughly.

"Today Munu was beaten by Ratnam," she said.

Munu, my youngest brother, slept on the wooden dais, cuddling himself. One cheek was bruised and swollen, his nose caked with snot. The other boys and girls were nowhere to be seen.

"Hey Ravi!" Letchumi called from her house, having seen me return. "Kamala stole rice from my pot. The thieving monkey! Why don't you tie her up?"

88 *The Return • Chapter Seven*

In the evening a quarrel raged between Letchumi and my mother. My father slapped the drunken Ratnam.

"I've gone to jail for beating up a man. I can go again," Ratnam threatened.

"Don't touch the children. Fight with another who drinks toddy," my father said.

"Eh, Kannan, why are your children buzzing about our houses like flies?" Govindan wanted to know.

My father sat stiffly at his table sucking on the black, fireless cigar.

Karupi stood in the doorway; I sat in the cubicle.

"Ravi didn't go to the laundry today," she said.

"Who beat you, Ravi?" my father said.

"My teacher gave me homework," I said.

"Who's going to give us food?" Karupi said.

"You want me to skin you?" my father said, turning on Karupi.

She went away to Mariamah and soon their laughter floated, through the thin walls, to us.

That year the Deepavali goats were not slaughtered. The children wore some of the newer clothes customers had sent in for washing. They were told not to leave the hospital compound or visit the other houses too long. Each child had been issued with only one round of crackers. We let them off early in the morning, after our bath, and while my brothers and sisters joined the other children in the long-house, I pored over a pile of frequently-fingered comics. At dinner time we shared out the remainder of the two chickens cooked for lunch.

The Annual Speech Day, grander than the ones I had known, was graced by Mr. Stockwell, the Chief Education Officer for Kedah. The variety concert had ground to a joyless end. Mr. Stockwell stood up. The Ah Huat Radio shop assistant tuned up the amplifier and the tall Englishman stood before the microphone.

"Ladies and gentlemen," he said, "it gives me great pleasure to be here this evening. When I first read the invitation to this occasion, I laughed. What school isn't English? I've spoken to the headmaster and we've decided to give this school distinction. Ha! Ha! I mean, distinction. From next year this school will be known as Tengku Mahkota in honour of His Highness, the Sultan. There will be another distinction – and this will have to be earned by the school. A Standard Six, state-level, examination will be introduced. So only the best will be admitted to Form One the year after. This school has to produce distinctions in order to rise above the unsung list of schools in the Education Department."

The adults clapped, the headmaster beamed, teachers frowned and those of us who would be in Standard Six the following year looked at each other with doubt and fear.

As I walked home in the dark, past the dimly-lit church, the silent playgrounds, and through the noisy streets of Sungai Petani, to the bus-stand, I felt I had at last surfaced from a mysterious, dark world. The year ahead stood like a rope bridge over a slimy, crocodile-infested river. Could I cross over to the other bank without falling to the snouts?

I quickened my pace, boarded a bus and reached home to await the new year.

8

Apparently, my parents too had made a new year resolve. My father slept later than usual: the house was relatively quiet. The children made no sound. There was an orderly clatter of plates and mugs. Munu didn't set up his usual morning wail. These peaceful mornings lasted a week. The money from the tapping must have been depleted for the children became clamorous again. The old scramble for breakfast was reinstated.

But the signs of prosperity didn't completely vanish. My two mothers prepared an elaborate feast the following week. At least three chickens were slaughtered. The gizzards, liver and heart were fried in chillies. The bones made up another crunchy plate. My father sent me to the town for half a dozen bottles of Stout. Bayi appeared and the first bottle was opened. My father shared a glass with him. We had sorted out the laundered and ironed clothes that evening. The numerous neat bundles were ranged about the room. The children, dressed in their finest, were fed early and sent to bed. As the eating progressed and the bottles emptied the Bayi smiled more and my father pointed to the clothes, mentioned Karupi and me. In some bewildering ritual, my father made me display my books and writing. Bayi gave me an arithmetic problem, which I solved without effort. I had to speak a few sentences in English.

My father woke up early next morning. He didn't sit, gazing at nothing, at the verandah table. The black cigar glowed. The children had been hushed; I was sent to Ah Chong's shop to buy toasted, *kaya*-spread slices of bread. Ah Chong's eyes widened when I handed him the ten-dollar note.

"Who can find the change so early in the morning?" he growled.

When my father had dressed in clean shorts and a well-ironed shirt, he looked at me.

"Get dressed. We're going to town," he said, a twinkle in his eyes.

I hadn't seen him so lively in months. I was excited as I got into my clothes. It was like old times: I sat on the carrier listening to his steady breathing. He had given me a white bundle to hold. The town came up like a revelation. We were rarely allowed to wander its streets, laid out in a square. Besides, we had been too busy. The town had grown. Behind the market had risen a zinc-roofed collection of houses, and facing the road itself, two rows of shophouses. My father stopped at one of them. An Indian, who had been waiting for him, smiled, then opened the large front door.

I had my first view of my father's laundry-shop in town. The front portion, a small hall, contained old glass cases, a broad desk and rattan chairs. The only room, adjacent to it, was three-quarters taken up by a table which could serve as a bed. A bathroom built over a well took up part of the long, gloomy back hall. And at the back, oblong and whitewashed, was the kitchen. At one corner was the bucket-latrine cubicle.

The man and my father talked terms while I rummaged about in the attic over the front hall. It could be a

---

kaya – Coconut jam.

comfortable hideout. My father called me. The man had disappeared and my father was already unwrapping the bundle.

"Get a small bottle of coconut oil," he said.

When I came back I saw a leaf-shaped, copper lamp in the corner, a framed picture of Lakshmi leaning against the wall.

"Light the lamp," he said.

Lakshmi, the goddess of wealth, rose out of the picture as the corner brightened.

Having lived mainly in the countryside, the thought of actually spending a night in town excited me. I was to sleep in the room behind the shop-front, make my own breakfast and leave for school as soon as Karupi arrived from the hospital compound. Though I would be alone at night, the new responsibility had two advantages. The noise in the hospital house would be absent, and I had a room to myself.

Business started a week after I lighted the lamp in the shop.

My first illusions about independence and leading a sophisticated life in town were soon destroyed. Karupi watched all my movements. On my return from school I ate the lunch brought from home in a tiffin-carrier. Then I did duty in the shop while Karupi napped. I couldn't read for half an hour without being interrupted.

"Ravi check if the bus driver's uniform is ready," Karupi said.

I rummaged in the glass cases for the clothes. There was no system. You had to remember the number of articles and their colours to locate them. Karupi made it a point to scrutinise the clothes the minute they were brought in.

"Not that one, Ravi. Khaki, not gray," she said, irritated.

I went back to the shelves.

"Yes, that bunch. Count and see if there are four," she said.

It was embarrassing watching her hunt for the clothes while customers waited.

"Not this one," she mumbled. "Did you send in two handkerchiefs?"

The customers smiled cynically.

"Don't you keep a list?" one said.

"We've always kept them in our heads," Karupi said proudly.

The man sniggered.

At the next sorting out of the clothes I introduced a more reliable identification system. My inspiration came from the Chinese laundries I had seen in Sungai Petani. Small slips of paper, with the receipt number and date, were placed in each bundle of sorted clothes. Karupi grumbled about not being able to read, so I put in the dhobi marks as well.

Our family was a work force, not a unit of affection, living together. My mother went to the laundry shed in the mornings, replacing Karupi. My grandmother trained my younger brothers and sisters to fetch the dry clothes in the afternoons. I attended to customers in the shop. My father worked in the laundry shed in the mornings and ironed in the shop during the afternoons.

The bulky figure of Bayi appeared at the shop frequently. I went out for the now customary bottle of Stout. He went away with ten or twenty dollars every time.

"Give him once a month," Karupi said.

"The empty drawer? Better remove the dirt little by little," my father said.

"He drinks too much," Karupi said.

"But he lent us the money," my father said.

One evening Karupi came back from the hospital compound looking crestfallen. I had been studying in the back room an hour or so, my father trying to get through that day's ironing. Around that time we had our tea but Karupi had to say the word first. Usually she washed the large yellow mug and took twenty cents from the drawer. Then she sent me to the corner coffeeshop. I came back with plain tea to which Karupi added the sugar and milk.

"Where's the tea?" my father asked.

Karupi sat in a rattan chair outside the shop staring at the empty mid-evening road.

"I said where's the tea?"

"What can tea do? We don't even have a future," Karupi said solemnly.

"Let's have the tea first," my father said.

He had put the flat irons on the stove, stoking the fire with a few lumps of coal. That would give him half an hour's respite from work.

"Tea! Tea! Tea! That's all you worry about! I've just come back from Ayah's house," Karupi said.

"That's not unusual. What did you and Amah gossip about today?"

"About that pig-eating boy of yours," she said. "He has our future in his hands."

"He has to grow up first, then work," my father said.

"He has to work now. The Amah said Ayah and the Big House are angry. They haven't seen Ravi for some time. They want him to deliver the clothes or they will send it to the Chinese laundry," Karupi said.

My father sat pulling at his cigar and rubbing his bare chest. The iron stove sparked and blazed.

"Why?" my father said at last.

"He's cleaner in his habits, they say," Karupi said. "Amah makes me sit on the bottom step instead of at the doorway."

"They should put you near the toilet," Father said.

The angry tone suggested he had come to a decision

much against his wishes. I would have to resume my
delivery duties. So I waited, as certain social laws in that
small town required, at the staircase of the hospital
bungalow and the Big House. The twice-a-week ordeal
eroded whatever self-confidence I had developed. They
always made me feel I was a dhobi's son and could never
dream of being more.

School work mounted. The automatic promotion of the
previous years had stolen the sense of urgency required for
examination preparation. It took discipline to get back into a
competitive mood. When I reached school by the last school
bus from Bedong, I saw my classmates already sitting in
rows against the classroom walls, poring over their books.
Mr. Veerasingham, our class teacher, was a tyrant for
efficiency. He took us in most subjects and they were all
competitions. Boys getting less than seven marks out of ten
were slapped. The spelling sessions were physical and
psychological tortures. We stood up beside our desks in
rows. He gave us each a word. If we got the spelling correct
we sat down. If we got it wrong the boy behind spelled it.
Then *he* slapped the boy who had erred. The arm had to
make its full swing or the correct-speller would be slapped
by Mr. Veerasingham.

During the first months in Standard Six, I dreaded
spelling periods. I was invariably slapped by my own
friends. I took to memorising words during recess, on the
way home in the bus, in between waiting on customers in
the shop. The slaps decreased but didn't stop completely.
My study time at home was being cut into by laundry duties.
I waited for closing time, which was never regular.
Sometimes we closed at eight, sometimes at nine-thirty. On
estate advance and pay days the shop remained open as late
as a quarter past ten. I took a chilling bath with the well
water and sat at my books until one.

Bayi showed up whenever he thought there was

money in the till. Usually he received some trifling
instalment and went, after guzzling a Stout, his way. There
was never enough money for the basics, let alone luxuries.
But Karupi had somehow placed the down-payment for a
battery-operated Grundig radio. It blared the whole day long
and the battery had to be replaced as often as once a week.

"Some entertainment in our dull lives," she explained
whenever customers complained of its loudness.

Our family was a regular hive of industry. My father
attended weddings, funerals and child-naming ceremonies.
In those days the white vesti served many functions: screen
over a corpse being washed, covering for the wedding dais,
and table cloth for feasts. On such days Karupi took over
the ironing and even my grandmother came in to do her bit.
For a while Karupi employed a young Chinese, who spoke
a little Tamil.

"Anyone who speaks our language can be trusted,"
Karupi intoned.

After a month Ah Kow disappeared with a batch of
expensive saris. We took a few months to compensate our
clients.

Karupi insisted I write out all the receipts and the tabs
for the sorted bundles of clothes. I could hardly move out of
the shop except on delivery errands.

The cycling into adjacent estates, the Indian homes
around Bedong, and money worries finally took their toll on
my father. He was sick for a week. Karupi conducted the
washing operations in the laundry shed. I ironed my first
clothes that week, recalling detail after detail of my father's
movements at the ironing table. When he took over after his
recovery, I went back to the studies I had neglected.

"What's that boy doing?" Karupi said. "I never knew he
could iron so well."

"He has an examination this year," my father said.

"A young boy can do both things – work and study,"

Karupi said. "Where's he now? Ravi?"

I came out of the room.

"Don't you want to improve your new skill?"

"I've got to study," I said.

"Study! Study! Study! Only an excuse to read your picture books!" she said angrily.

"Leave him alone! He has done enough work," my father said.

"Yes, spoil him. The barber next door tells me the lamp is on until one in the morning," Karupi said. "Reading those picture books will turn his head."

Karupi's insistence increased; I stayed back in school more often. Shutting myself up in an empty classroom, I went through the homework, revised that week's lessons and then walked to the bus-stand to take the evening bus home. I only got slapped occasionally during the spelling bees. Arithmetic, which had become more complex, wasn't difficult any more. My confidence in the other subjects increased as well. Some of the fear for the final examination disappeared.

The situation at home, however, hadn't improved. Though my mother didn't have to trudge through the early morning to Riverside Estate, she still looked haggard. My grandmother returned later and later to the house. The children were left to their own devices. The few hours I returned home, mainly for dinner, I saw we had fallen in social prestige.

One evening, as I passed the bungalow, the gardener hailed me.

"The Ayah wants to see you," he said.

I went through the usual waiting before the man condescended to see me. He had balded at the front and looked more sinister. The limp was pronounced; he used a stick around the house. He leaned on it as he descended the few steps into the newly-added sitting room. He stood a long time, looking at me.

"What do you read at school?" he said.

"Usual text-books," I said.

"Story books?"

"Some," I said recalling my library hours.

"Why are you late coming back home almost every day?"

"Not every day," I said.

"Why?"

"I study in a classroom," I said.

He laughed.

"You've a home. And a shop. No place to study?"

"Too much noise and work!"

"So, getting above your station, ah?" he said malevolently. "See how that family's suffering. Even I let them run a business. They don't wash the hospital clothes properly. I close one eye."

I waited to be dismissed. His children stood in the doorway suppressing their giggles. Then he turned towards the steps.

"Don't bring misfortune to your family with your book ideas," he said.

The gravel crunched under my feet as I walked back to the laterite road. Until I reached the junction of the main road I was unable to think. A dark helplessness overpowered me. The shop, when I reached it, looked so miniature, every piece of wood and zinc fragile and exposed.

The year drew to a close. Tengku Mahkota was gearing itself for the task of producing the best students in the district. The school was a prolonged hum of learning. Teachers worked harder; students had a strained, determined look.

Towards the end of the year, the shop was partitioned off by a low wooden wall. Pather, that Bedong legend, occupied the long, narrow room. He had placed a two-inch platform, on which rested his desk and the stoves, on the floor. The man had changed: the scar on his throat wobbled whenever he spoke. I had a companion during the nights. His devotional songs kept me awake so that I concentrated on my school work. When I made coffee I gave him some; he always thanked me politely. My father got clearer reports about my night working habits.

The rest passed me in a haze. The children cried more, my mother became gaunt, my grandmother's wiry strength succumbed — she slept early — and Karupi went visiting Amah frequently. Bayi hovered constantly, like an apparition, in the glass showcases. I recall my father opening the drawer, brooding, then handing over red, green and blue notes. Once the Bayi stood in the shop doorway refusing to move until my father had "something" for him. My father placed tattered, dirty, one-dollar notes before the man. Bayi took them and turned away, muttering.

Then the examination week rushed past. Soon we were listening to the teachers' advice on our future.

School closed. I never left the shop. The comics and books I had saved for reading after the examination filled the lull during that month. The Grundig was silent, the battery gone fungoid. Karupi rarely remained in the shop. I opened the shop, ironed clothes, sorted and laid them out on the shelves, wrapped bundles for customers.

Suddenly a Chinese classmate of mine appeared.

"You passed!" he said.

I forgot to move the iron and there was a smell of a faintly burnt shirt.

"Fourth in the State," he said.

For the first time since I had been running the shop, I took a couple of dollars from the drawer and, informing Pather, left with my friend.

We sat, I remember, in a coffeeshop, hardly touching

the koay teow soup we had ordered. We belonged to
Tengku Mahkota's new elite!

"So you've grown wings!" Karupi said when I returned
after putting my friend on a Sungai Petani-bound bus. "If the
clothes had been stolen?"

"I passed my Standard Six examination," I said.

My father, when he heard the news, didn't say
anything, but his face showed he was pleased. That evening
he gave me a five-dollar note.

"Buy whatever you want," he said.

As the school days approached I noticed a strange
silence in the home and the shop. My mother was silent at
meal times. My father seemed preoccupied with work in the
shop. Only Karupi displayed a smile.

At closing time I was assigned the duty of counting the
day's takings and allocating money for coal, starch, soap and
food. Karupi hardly touched the receipt book though she
had a smattering of Tamil.

"Ravi, see what the man wants," she said in Tamil
whenever a customer walked into the shop.

She was content to sit in the rattan chair near the
partition, talking about local affairs to the goldsmith, who
merely grunted.

When I started putting my books together and ironed
my school uniform, Karupi looked triumphantly at me.

"You're not going to school," she said.

"Something important to do?" I said.

"No more schooling for you," she said.

My head flooded with anger.

"Why not?"

"The Ayah says so," she said. "Go and see him."

I went to school anyway. My grandmother gave me the
bus fare and that month's fees. The afternoon was still when
I returned that day.

"You've become a big man, is that it?" Karupi said.

"You've studied enough. You know how to read and write. Now you can take full charge of the shop."

My father turned from the ironing table, face worn out with some kind of a conflict. There was that pride that he had shown during the initiation ceremony before I went to the Tamil school, but also defeat.

"We've little money to send you to school," he said.

I sat at the desk looking at the receipt book for a long time.

The next day, on an impulse, I went into the school office and inquired about scholarships. There was one offered by the Indian High Commission. I filled in the forms then and there, found Mr. Veerasingham to stand as referee, and returned home with misgivings. My grandmother, when I went to her in the evening, promised to see me through secondary school.

"Old bones and skin. Something it can live for now," she said.

We were summoned by the Ayah. He scrutinised both of us and spoke to my father first.

"Kannan, I understand your problems. I've also to maintain my position. How can I let you work in other places without earning disrespect and disobedience from the labourers?"

"I'm sorry to put you in this situation, Ayah," my father said.

"I've spoken to that son of yours," he said, "but he won't listen. Nowadays a little education goes to the head. He might even think of becoming a doctor and order me about."

"No, no, Ayah," my father protested.

"We've to stop such useless dreams. I'm told he has boxes of comics and story books in his room. You should have controlled him earlier."

"I don't read English, Ayah," my father said.

Something in his voice gave me courage. Ayah turned to me.

"You should be grateful your father has educated you so far. Now be a dutiful son and help the family."

"You want me to stop going to school?" I said.

"See how he talks without respect, Kannan?" Ayah appealed to my father.

"I hope I don't offend you, Ayah, but I've something to say. I know how you help me. But I can't stop the boy. Nor will I support him. If he finds the money and goes to school, he must be allowed to do so," my father said.

The Ayah smiled.

"That's a good way to bring this upstart back to his senses," he said.

A month later I received news that I had been granted the scholarship. There was enough to pay the fees, buy the monthly bus pass, and uniforms which would last a year.

9

The victory, my father's and mine over Ayah, had a strange effect on the people of Bedong and on my family's fortunes. My father, whom I had now begun to call *Naina* (the filial honorific in Telugu), earned a new reputation in the town. Even the Malays and Chinese nodded to him, softly uttering the word 'Ayah', a general form of according respect. I learned to live under the peoples' censure and envy. Ganesh didn't hurl 'White monkey' at me any more.

When I cycled past Menon's house some evenings, to have my dinner and visit my mother, I saw Menon's wife at the window, glaring at me. She quickly summoned her children to her side.

"Dhobi's son! Dhobi's son!" they jeered.

I averted my face and pedalled even faster past the bend. On my way back I would hear the black, large Alsatian growl at me from the driveway, but the monster's impotent pawing behind the locked gates only made me smile in the dark.

"You don't come home to me enough," my mother said as she served the meal.

She washed the porcelain plate she used only for me before heaping it with rice, potatoes, and a whole fried fish

---

Naina – Telugu word for 'Father'.

she had saved for me.

"Work," I mumbled.

"I'm not important to you anymore. I've nothing to offer except your meals," she said, sitting beside me.

"Don't you want me to do well at school?" I said.

"When are you coming again?"

"Next year," I said, glad to get away.

Ratnam would be returning soon to trigger off the drunken brawls, the flinging of filthy curses and a fight or two. The long-house children were already clamouring for their night meal, their mothers standing in the lighted doorways, gossiping. I left at about the time the children started banging plates and mugs. As I reached the corner the lights from the long-house caught me, suddenly, from over the shoulder. But I rode blindly down the slope, taunting Menon's Alsatian.

From the day I saw that room adjacent to the shop, I took full possession of it. No one, not even Naina could step over the threshold without some kind of approval from me. I had had neither the time nor the money to improve its looks. But after I began receiving the scholarship money, I spent some of it changing the room's decor. Good wall paper was expensive, so I plastered the walls with plain, brown paper. On each of the walls I hung a framed poster of the English countryside, particularly of 'daffodil land'. There were shelves now, nailed on the supporting beams of the walls, and they held many books. Biggles had ceased to interest me; Wallace, H.G. Wells, Thackeray and Dickens replaced my former reading tastes. They were mostly abridged and simplified versions, but the pleasure wasn't diminished.

I read avidly, sitting at an ornately carved desk or lying down on the camp bed. The first year of my secondary school life passed away pleasantly, with plenty to read and the time to enjoy my own company. Occasionally, Mike, from the hospital staff quarters, dropped in. He was in my class and he introduced me to Mickey Spillane, Agatha Christie, Erle Stanley Gardner and P.G. Wodehouse. We spent many afternoons sipping some bottled drinks and marvelling over Bertie Wooster's adventures. Sometimes I visited Mike in his house, when I felt I had had enough of the solitary evenings, and when I could outstare Mrs. Menon.

Karupi, my stepmother, hardly said anything or stopped any of my activities. There were periods during the day when I had to do some duty in the shop. Karupi would be, at such times, in the makeshift kitchen at the back or gone to the barber shop, to deliver clothes and chat. Naina wouldn't have come in from the hospital laundry shed. The work wasn't difficult. The system I had started was still retained and I took some pleasure in wrapping up the clothes for customers or writing out a receipt in English.

We had come out from the stormy passage in our difficulties. Bayi always went away satisfied, though I thought I detected a certain regret in his words:

"For how long can I drink your beer, Kannan?" he said to Naina on one occasion. ·

"As long as I'm in your debt," Naina said.

"And that won't be for long," Bayi said.

Naina put the flat iron down with some satisfaction on the asbestos resting board.

By the end of that year Bayi stopped appearing at the shop on pay and advance days. He did come, wiping his face, to rest his stumpy legs on the bench outside the shop whenever he shopped for the odd thing in town.

"You've another showcase now, Kannan," he said, giving the shop the once-over. "And that's a nice, big radio too."

The Grundig, Karupi's proud contribution to the shop, blared continuously, the batteries replaced as quickly as they lost their power. She would silently continue sorting out the clothes even if I fiddled with the tuning knob to get the BBC. I never left the shop on the days the "Goon Show" went on the air. One evening the battery was so weak the tiny indicator bulb wouldn't go on. Karupi placed eight dollars, the price of a new battery, in my hands.

Naina, working with renewed zest, piled shirt after shirt on the ironing table, the coal stove on which he warmed the flat irons glowing blue. When the rhythm took him he would finish as many as eighty pieces in a single evening. He stood on a foot-wide, smooth plank in front of the table, only the hands moving over the clothes or manipulating the iron. His right hand guided the iron, the left smoothed the wrinkles. Half-way through a shirt, he stopped, twirled around, clanged the irons changing them, and turned the garment into a glossy, crisp creation you could store in a biscuit tin. During such moods, a faint whistle resembling the rich, haunting melody from a Jew's harp, issued from his lips.

"Shut that cackle off! This shirt will wrinkle itself under such noise!" Naina said.

Karupi looked sadly at me; I turned off the radio. Though I retired to my room I waited for the rhythm to come through the thin walls. While the reassuring smell of roasted starch and damp cloth filled the air and that whistle produced its zinging swells, I sat in the room absorbing almost completely whatever I read.

I longed, however, to be taken over by Naina's mood, for he seemed such a modulated series of self-sustaining movements. And when he finished for the day, he sat a long time on the bench outside, content and unreachable. I stood near the chicks, gazing at the bicycle and pedestrian traffic on the wide road. The roar from the toddy shop, behind the Chinese coffeeshop to the left, clashed with the deep silence over Naina.

"I didn't want to shout like that," Naina said suddenly.

"The radio was too loud," I said.

"Your stepmother tells me you don't want to go to the Big House with the clothes," he said gently.

"Yes," I said.

"You must listen to what your head tells you," he said. "I'll send Samy."

Samy, four years younger than I, had one day simply refused to attend the primary English school facing the main road. He hung around the Chinese bicycle-repair shops, mending punctures and changing spokes for the experience. Samy pestered Naina to have the old bicycle remodelled, but my father shook his head. The bicycle had served well and was too much in demand just then to be put in Samy's tampering hands.

"He'll have to pay for the rice he eats at home," Naina said.

Kumar, an even younger brother, shouldered most of the delivery duties. The girls helped mainly in the laundry shed, keeping my grandmother company. In the evenings they clustered round my mother, lightening her cooking and washing chores. I hardly knew them. Whenever I went to the hospital house for my meals, they kept a good distance away from me. They had forgotten how my grandmother and I had looked after them when Mother and Karupi had gone tapping in Riverside Estate. Karupi, who sometimes went to the laundry shed leaving me in charge of the shop, must have instructed them well. They had all dropped out of school in favour of the mindless work and the beguiling chatter around the laundry shed and the kitchen fire.

Karupi had just got back from the hospital compound. Naina was due in two hours. Karupi glanced around the shop, thumbed through the receipt book and looked at Pather who was napping over his work desk in that narrow cubicle. She noticed the brown package on the large desk.

"What's that, Ravi?" she said.

"Some clothes I ironed for an urgent customer," I said.

"The clerk in the post office?"

"Yes."

"I was waiting for your father to come and do them," she said.

"I had finished reading. The man needed them at once," I said.

The man came in then, an aggressive air about him.

"Finished?" he said.

"Yes," I said, handing him the package.

"The work is good but you're not fast enough. Tell your father that," he said and walked briskly away.

"You know your responsibilities, Ravi," Karupi said, a faint trace of admiration in her voice.

I looked away. She slid the money the customer had left on the table into the drawer.

"I've just come from Ayah's house," she said. "They talked a lot about you. Don't you wear shorts any more, they said. Don't you feel like a girl hiding in this shop, they said. They don't know you now wear trousers, not shorts."

Pather came out of his snooze. He looked at her incredulously and bent over his work, shaking his head. When Karupi went to the back he nodded to me, a pair of unbelieving eyes gazing over the bifocals he had begun to wear.

"Why is she speaking like that now?" he said. "A snake has two tongues."

"I don't know," I said, bewildered by Karupi's change.

She was the first to inquire about my examination results that year. Form One was a difficult class; the syllabus emphasized self-discovery, especially in the science subjects. Though fascinated by the physics classes, I wasn't entirely comfortable in them. The interpretations of the readings from the various instruments confused me. My conclusions weren't always accurate though my neat writing out of the experiments and the graphic diagrams drew praise from the teachers. I was placed somewhere in the middle of the class that year. But Karupi, who had seen the proliferation of print and illustrations in the hard-cover books I brought home was full of encouragement.

"In my heart of hearts I knew you would do well," she said.

"You've only passed," Naina said. "Govindan talked to me at the laundry this morning. Ganesh is last in class. Ayah's son is getting the State prize."

The ironing table shook as he put the iron down hastily. The flames in the stove jumped, orange and red. The air smoked.

"You've to think of other things too," Naina said.

He didn't stay in the shop the entire evening. And when he went out it wasn't to a wedding or funeral with a supply of white vestis. His bicycle stood near the drain, under the umbrella tree, late into the night. Karupi had tied up the bundles of dirty clothes for the laundry, washed the tiffin carrier in readiness for the walk back to the hospital house. Naina returned looking a trace dishevelled and smoking a cigarette, something I had never seen him do.

Naina didn't say a word for a week. I came back from school one afternoon with a cheque for ninety-six dollars, the second half-yearly scholarship remittance. I went up to the ironing table over which he was bent, pressing a particularly difficult piece, the folded, gold-bordered, silk wedding thundu. Bridegrooms wore the thundu across the front, over a silk *jubbah*, as they bent to tie the thali round their bride's neck. The end of the thundu had to be displayed, spreading out stiff and fan-wise. People often made scathing remarks if the thundu didn't "perform".

---

jubbah – Loose, long-sleeved shirt.

I placed the cheque, where he could see it, beside the pile of pressed clothes. He didn't speak until he had "tested" the thundu, holding it upright so that the ends fell into a wonderful fountain of controlled silk. There was a wisp of a smile on Naina's lips.

"What do you have to show me?" he said, seeing the cheque for the first time. "Money? Keep it. There's something else in life."

The cheque lay there, gradually losing its gloss under the spray of water Naina applied to the clothes, the whole evening. In the end, Karupi intervened.

"Take the money. Remember he fought for it when you couldn't afford his school fees," she said.

"It's his money. Let him keep it," Naina said.

"He has always given it to you. And asked for whatever he wanted," Karupi said. "Don't put salt in the milk."

Karupi handed the cheque to me a few days later.

"He asks you to keep the money required for next year's fees, bus fare and clothes. The rest you can spend. Buy some things for yourself," Karupi said.

"I want to buy a cupboard for my books," I said.

"Buy it. You've the money now," Karupi said.

"I won't have enough for school expenses," I said.

"Buy it," she said. "I'll give you the money at the end of the month."

The cupboard stood, a week later, in the corner of my room at the head of the camp bed. I could easily select, looking through the glass doors, the book I wanted to read before sleeping. The two drawers above the shelves held an adolescent's secret hoards and articles that evoked passion. When later I affixed "James" to Ravi and corresponded with British and American pen-pals, the letters, particularly from girls, lay nestling among the stamp albums and glass ball of confetti snow. James Ravi lived in the drawers, emerging at night, when the shop was closed, my parents gone back to the hospital house.

Karupi made up, as she had promised, the deficit in the scholarship allowance, at the end of the month.

"Your father has strange dreams, but he has a generous heart," she said.

I felt I had, at last, come into my own, my family incapable of understanding my dreams, but full of sympathy for them.

10

Bedong had been changing. The old shopkeepers who had depended solely on the personal touch, that is, knowing a particular group of people through family and social contacts for a clientele, had to adopt a more progressive attitude. They were unable to keep out the travelling salesmen who conducted business on the roadside in front of their own shops. These salesmen went round the estates, kampungs, even the streets of Bedong itself, blaring their attractive offers on their loudspeakers. In the evenings they set up their aluminium shelves; bright fluorescent bulbs, connected to large batteries, threw an alluring gloss on their wares. Shoes, bedsteads, rolls of cloth heaped into a small mountain, fell with seductive folds and colours to the tarmac. The men, in their loosened shirt-necks and awry ties, spoke endlessly into hailers. The Malay woman I had known to have a crowd around her hand-woven mats, reed bags and caskets, sat silently munching on her sireh. The potter, who had cast his vessels in a semi-covered shed behind Periathai's house, arranged his pots, *kualis*, jars, calabashes, in pyramidal fashion, as he had always done, beside the light-radiating aluminium wares of the mobile van-shops. Only a few people bent down (and these mainly from the estate), to hold a clay pot in their hands and to

kualis –Deep, frying pans.

knock with their knuckles for that perfect, resounding ring.

The old shop facades came down. Planks that had served as shutters, each numbered and slotted into a wooden groove, the door detached and assembled every morning and evening, were slowly replaced by the iron grille. The garishly-painted wooden windows on the rooms above the shops were removed. Now, in the evening sunlight, you had to shade your eyes against the glare the glass threw at you. Painted signboards appeared at the shop fronts, logos in a select few. The Eng Hin Electric Company had begun supplying the town only that year.

Before the town shut down for the night, under curfew regulations, at eleven, it had, almost every day, a festival air. A tin shed cinema, built beside the fenced off post office, screened a show each evening, at six-thirty. Cinema-goers crowded the coffeeshops before and after the film. Even under the curfew hours, though these had been relaxed over the previous three years, the town had gradually but inevitably become the centre of our lives. *Mee* stalls sprang up between the now-rebuilt rows of shophouses. A steadier, constant flow of people and traffic filled the wide streets. A shoe-repairer set up his stand at the pillar opposite Periathai's, on the pawnshop verandah. Mary Mangalam, a railway official's widow, opened (a revolutionary move), a book-shop on the main road. The shop, brightly-lit and showcases filled with trashy Tamil novels, buzzed more with curious visitors then genuine buyers. Her two daughters, well developed and sociable for their age, never left the glass counter.

Karupi sighed as she sorted the dirty linen and threw the "marked" ones into a commodious wooden box. Naina briskly turned out article after ironed article. He didn't have coffee breaks now, drinking from the mug as his hands

---

mee – Noodles.

wielded the flat irons. The hissing of the gaslight, suddenly "gulping" as the impurities in the capillary tube blocked the oil, irritated Karupi.

"I can't do anything under this fickle light!" she said.

Naina went on working. Karupi put down the seed from which she extracted a black juice for marking the clothes with a needle.

"Look at these fingers! The lime is making a sore," she said.

The bottle of the liquid she dipped into and dabbed over the black marks, to fix them, shot from her hands. Customers sometimes complained of smudged collars and handkerchief corners.

"What do you really want?" Naina said, turning at last to her.

"You've been listening!" Karupi said. "We've got to change some things in this shop. People will go back to the Chinese dhobi if we do business in a cave."

The gaslight gulped; Pather uttered a soft curse in the sudden, brief darkness.

"We must put in electric light," Karupi said.

"All right," Naina said. "Don't bring in a dozen other improvements."

I helped Naina fill in the application forms; I read under a naked bulb in my room a fortnight later. Installing electricity was a needed improvement. The shop attracted more of the cinema crowd; they stood, sometimes, outside the shop, gazing at the trousers and a few coats on hangers in the glass showcases. Pather had a few, apparently well-to-do, women watching him fashion an ear-ring.

"I didn't know that these new-fangled kinds of lighting attracted people like moths," he told Naina.

"I've ironed more clothes than before," Naina said.

Karupi entered a frenzied mood of innovation. I don't know how she juggled the finances, but the shop got a new coat of paint.

"Aren't lights enough?" Naina said.

"They show up the cracks and cobwebs," Karupi said.

"Why all the ply-wood wall?"

"We're not goats penned in cages. Now Pather can have his own cubicle," Karupi said.

She had extended the half-wall separating us and Pather up to the ceiling, leaving a side door through which he could go to the bathroom and kitchen. A high, formica-topped counter with compartments for wrapping paper, newly received linen, receipt books, drawers for money and important documents, stood beside the main showcase. She also made me design a logo and wording for the shop. The Indian boy who painted signs soon had "Mynah Cleaners" displayed over the front, above the recently-hung red-and-pink chicks.

"Every day I come to a new shop," Naina said, but went on with his work.

People didn't stop only to gaze at the painted sign and gaily displayed, pressed clothes in the showcases. They came with bundles, at first distrustfully and coyly, then with greater regularity and confidence. Karupi placed me behind the counter most of the evenings. My hands soon became skilled at making up the parcels, expertly snipping off that inch-length tape for the finished look. Karupi had readily agreed to my suggestion to use tape instead of string.

The hours immediately after lunch were the quietest and the least busy. Pather too downed his tools and now, hidden from us by the high wall, napped over his desk. Karupi stretched out in the hall, across my room, and snored. Only when the radio went off at three did life stir in the shops down the row. Then long shadows slanted across the road; the bicycle shop began clinking and hissing. A few voices came from the provision shops beside ours. A group of Indians went past to be first in the queue at the toddy shop.

Lorries trundled down the road to Tanjung Dawai, to collect the fish. The bus service between that fishing village and Bedong resumed with a grind of gears. Customers began to stream into the shop. When Naina arrived he had to do the pieces that had been sent in only for pressing. By then I was busy at the counter or moving between the showcases, peering up the shelves, locating a particular customer's washing and bundling it up. Karupi sorted out clothes the customers brought in. I wrote out the receipts; she received the money. After tea, which was now ordered from the coffeeshop down the road, I sorted out the washed and ironed clothes, tabbed and arranged them on the shelves. Kumar came in for the clothes that had to be delivered to various houses. Karupi tied these up, giving him detailed instructions. I went off to the back, bathed and read for a while.

The noise of quarrels from the toddy stall, haggling in the sundry shops along ours, and the early cinema patrons, the harsh crashing of gears, rose and fell beyond my room. Then suddenly the road became silent. My meal – I went only occasionally to the house in the hospital grounds – would have been brought in a tiffin-carrier, and Karupi knocked on my door.

"We're going home, Ravi," she said.

I came out. Naina was bundling huge piles of clothes which he and Kumar loaded on their bicycles. Karupi counted the day's takings, gave me my pocket money and wrapped the rest in a handkerchief. The shop felt empty after they had left. Only Pather's chanting of some devotional song interrupted the silence. Some Chinese took a walk before the curfew siren went.

We were making money. The food had improved; there was chicken at least once a week. Sometimes I stopped at the Cold Storage in Sungai Petani, on my way back from school, and bought five pounds of imported mutton.

At the end of one month, I asked for a bedstead. Neither Karupi nor Naina objected. The room was complete and comfortable. Entering it was being transported into a world different from the one I spent my daylight hours in. The sight of the new, flowered wallpaper, painting of a yacht and the poster of pine trees on a rocky landscape, the sun a sparkling, ephemeral ball, lighted up a pleasant, opportunity-filled world within me.

11

That year curfew, reduced by two hours, was imposed only between 12 and 5 a.m. The cinema screened two shows, at 5.30 and 8.30 p.m. Shops remained open an hour later. Naina, Karupi and Kumar delayed their return to the hospital house. I could sometimes catch the nine-thirty bus from Sungai Petani, after an evening English film. The Majestic in Bedong screened mainly Chinese, Malay and Indian films. People moved about with less fear. An army unit was stationed at Merbok, a dozen miles from Bedong, for a military exercise. Naina had contracted to do its laundry.

The green jeep stopped at the shop twice a week. I came out to talk to the driver, count the clothes and check my numbers with his. We talked in English. Naina looked unhappy whenever he sorted through the green uniforms and bundled them up for the laundry shed in the hospital.

"I don't know what Ayah will say," he said.

"You've nothing to be afraid of. The hospital clothes are always done properly and returned on the correct days," Karupi said.

"You don't have to be in the wards. His eyes seem to be full of fire," Naina said. "And I always have to fold my arms whenever he inspects a bundle."

"What's cringing before that man if we feed our children well," Karupi said.

On the rare occasions I cycled to the hospital, always
now under the cover of dusk, I hoped I wouldn't be
stopped on the way. The boys were there, on the field
between the long-house and Menon's bungalow, a game of
some sort in progress. They looked at me with hostility or
made remarks which I couldn't catch for the shouting
among the younger children.

A passion for gardening had swept through the long-
house. My younger brothers and sisters, following their
neighbours, had some new plant or fruit to show me
whenever I got home.

"Look at the avarakai panthal!" Kumar said.

He led me to the vegetable plot. In the failing light I
saw the creepers, trellised, and laden with the light-green
legumes. Whole bunches hung from the rough, wooden
framework Kumar had put up for the plant.

"The custard apple is no good. Each one shrivels up,"
he commented.

I looked to the left where Kumar had ambitiously tried
groundnuts: a brown patch covered the furrows, the leaves
curled and tangled.

"The inspector has come!" Ganesh said, if he was
watering the plants in the adjacent plot.

He had dammed the large, common drain into which
all kinds of filth flowed. He and his brothers filled up their
pails with the scummy water and carried them carefully to
the furrows.

"Don't spill unnecessarily! Pour only on the roots!"
Ganesh commanded.

He stank now of the rot that had seeped into the long-
house. The cubicle-like houses had begun to flake their
green paint. Some pillars, exposed to the rain, had gone
hollow just above the cement base. The old-fashioned
humped tiles had cracked where twigs from the cotton or
rain trees had fallen. On rainy days the roof leaked. The

small generator that served the entire hospital compound supplied only feeble light through the forty-watt bulbs that hung over the two rooms in each house. The floors were badly pitted.

"You don't talk to your old friends!" Ganesh said.

"I've no time," I said.

"Running from cinema to cinema?"

"You don't give me the money," I said.

"You get enough washing peoples' dirty clothes," he said.

"I still smell clean," I said.

He came nearer and sniffed.

"Soap from England?"

I came away quickly. His father never allowed him out of the house the moment he came back from school. But I occasionally saw him gambling in the private school compound, a mile from Tengku Mahkota. He had done badly in the Standard Six Examination.

His father stood in his doorway watching us both. In my adolescent eyes he looked shabby. His usually white shirt had been dyed blue too heavily to hide the frayed seams, his shorts hung limp and bunched at his knees. The nose looked pronounced in a fatigued face.

"The new jamindar's son has come for a visit, Letchumi," he said to his wife. "Want to fall at his feet and ask for advice?"

"I didn't say anything to you," I said.

"I hope you haven't given my son your smooth, corrupted ways," he said. "I pray to God every day that my son recognises his parents and elders."

"How can he talk to you?" his wife said from inside. "The golden tongue may wear away."

"Why do you speak about my son like that?" my mother, called from our house. "He's only a boy. He has done you no harm."

"Are you a mother? Don't you know what he has inside his shorts?" Govindan said, properly launched now.

"Muruga! Muruga!" my mother said. "Don't you have any shame?"

"Shame is something money doesn't allow you to feel," Letchumi, a disembodied voice, said.

"You people don't know anything!" I shouted.

"Ravi, let through the other ear what these people say," my mother pleaded.

"People? Once we were your neighbours," Govindan said.

"Give me my dinner, Mother. I'm leaving all this filth behind," I said.

"Ravi! Ravi!" my mother begged.

Govindan went on as if I hadn't said anything. The scavenging for food among the children had been temporarily delayed. I felt ears cocked for whatever insults Govindan would heap on me.

"Even Ayah, who knows white man's knowledge had time to listen to us," Govindan said.

Then almost as if they had grown impatient of such triviality the children set up their clatter for food. My mother laid out my meal. I ate hurriedly.

"Don't worry about them. Come and see me as often as you can," my mother said.

My sisters were gathered in the other room, talking gaily and laughing.

"Eat!" my mother commanded. "Food gives courage."

My mother had lived for so long under Karupi's shadow that she was strange when she was alone. She had begun to mystify me. I wondered how she could stomach the filthy language, the evil plotting and gossiping that went

---

Muruga – The common name for God, used by Indians.

on in the long-house. And before I left she placed a dash of
thurnuru on my forehead, taken from the tray at the house
shrine. I stood before her, stiff and irritated.

As I pedalled away from the long-house, the sense of
humiliation and the need to escape mounted. My mother's
last image – an isolated, lonely figure in the dimly-lighted
doorway – sharpened this feeling. When I reached the bend
I almost jumped out of the bicycle saddle. A brutal keening
assaulted my ears. I caught glimpses of crouched figures
fluttering hands over mouths. The sound reached an
intolerable, piercing screech. I had been away so long in
town that I had forgotten that the guava trees provided
perfect hiding places for any kind of attack.

"White backside! Town filth!"

"Man with nothing between the legs!"

"Perfumed prostitute!" Ganesh's voice rose above the
others.

Trembling, frightened and angry I spat in the direction
of the trees and felt the bicycle chain tighten with my
urgency as I pedalled furiously towards the town.

Karupi smiled at me whenever I returned from the
hospital house and we would talk. But that night she felt my
coiled-up sense of violation and kept to herself. I stayed in
my room, reading the letters from my pen-pals or just staring
at the walls. The posters offended me; I felt impotent. When
Karupi knocked on the door to signal Naina's and her
departure, I didn't come out.

Naina was silent and preoccupied the following day.
Karupi busied herself at the counter; the radio was silent.
The irons were banged down with brutal regularity. Even
before Karupi switched on the shop lights, Naina had left. A
few hours later he showed up at the hospital house. Kumar,
frightened and awed, cycled up with the news. Karupi

---

thurnuru – White ash rubbed over the forehead on sacred occasions.

packed up immediately.

Naina didn't appear at the shop for a week. Karupi and I managed the business, using a temporary ironing hand, as usual. I stood at Naina's place, the high, well-padded ironing table, doing the shirts and trousers as well as I could. The work fascinated me enough to make me forget the undercurrent of tension within the family.

I returned from school one afternoon to find Kumar behind the counter.

"Where's stepmother?" I asked.

"Gone to the washing place," he said.

The food Kumar had brought in the tiffin carrier didn't possess my mother's customary spicy touch. The dhal and gravy hardly mixed, the rice was bloated and soggy, the fried fish burnt.

"What's happening, brother?" Kumar asked.

"I don't know," I said.

I took over at the counter and sent Kumar back. He was glad to go. A few minutes after his departure Karupi and Naina arrived. They were talking heatedly.

"I'm not ready to beg," Naina said, the black cigar held clenched between his teeth. "You were not there when he came. I had to hide the army uniforms. Yet he dug them out."

"Big people are like that. They want to know everything," Karupi said.

Naina, instead of changing his shirt for a singlet as he usually did, sat in a rattan chair, relaxed.

"Ravi has been doing your work," Karupi said.

"So you've come back, Kannan," Pather said from the other side of the wall.

Naina dug into his pockets, brought out a dollar and handed it to me.

"Bring me tea and some cigars," he said.

Naina sat a long time, sipping the tea and smoking the

cigars while I pressed some shirts, shyly, at his table. Karupi sorted the newly-laundered clothes, then went through the receipt books.

"Look at the people who send clothes to us now," she said, turning at last to Naina.

"Let them take their clothes to the Chinese," he said.

No one talked the rest of the evening. The pile on the table, when I had finished for the day, was considerable. Kumar rode up. Karupi placed bundles of dirty linen on the carrier and sent him on.

The long awaited storm broke. Naina came punctually with Karupi but still occupied that rattan chair, smoking away complacently. Kumar rode between the hospital house and the shop frenziedly, carting away the dirty clothes and bringing in the fresh ones for ironing. I stood patiently at the ironing table, my feet at last firmly feeling the grain of the smooth footboard.

"How can you sit there for so many days doing nothing?" Karupi burst out.

"What's a family for?" Naina said. "You're all doing fine. You don't need me."

"That's the smell of sour milk," Karupi said. "Come out straight with whatever you want to say."

"No one likes honesty nowadays," Naina said. "I told Ayah we've a large family and need the extra work."

"Too direct," Karupi said. "Look at Govindan. He wants to buy a gold chain for his wife, he consults the Ayah. Pretends he will buy just enough, won't outshine Amah's own necklace or bangles. See the collection Letchumi has now. Can open a jewelry shop."

"How long can a man fold his arms before another?" Naina said. "Hurt the knee from kneeling?"

"It's all for our own good," Karupi said. "I still accept the watered-down tea the Amah gives me."

"They simply don't want Ravi to attend an English

school," said Naina. "Look at how the boys insult him."

"I can take it," I said.

"We don't have to. From now on I'll only do the hospital work," he said.

"I've lost respect for that man!" Naina thundered the next day. "If he comes nosing round the laundry how can I do any work?"

"He likes you to beg," Karupi said. "Pretend a little."

"I don't understand him. I even said I'll pay for the extra water bill," Naina said.

"Start another laundry at the back of the shop," Karupi said.

"It's the same thing. We're still afraid of the man."

Naina came by himself from the hospital the following day; he sat hunched in the rattan chair. Karupi came panting and sweating in the face.

"You haven't done anything rash, I hope," she asked Naina.

He didn't look up. When he did his face had regained a former liveliness. He lighted a cigar.

"He scolded me in the office, in front of all those people," he said. "I won't bend my knee to any one any more."

"Amah said no one has spoken back to the Ayah," Karupi said. "Why did you shout at him?"

"Don't wag your twin-forked tongue!" Naina said. "Now you want me to obey him, now you instigate me against him! I won't work under him!"

Karupi remained silent. That evening, after counting the money, she kept some in the drawer, the key to which never left her.

Naina saw the landlord. When he came back, four hours later, his eyes sparkled. He had me get him a bottle of beer from the nearby coffeeshop. As he drank the beer he kept up a steady stream of talk.

"The man has allowed me to build the laundry," he told Karupi. "But he also wants rooms added."

"Why does he want rooms?" Karupi said.

"Where are the children going to sleep?" Naina asked. "This shop is going to be our home."

"And when we have put up the rooms, he will throw us out," Karupi said. "I don't like him at all."

"Then we will move into a real house!" Naina said, laughing.

The laundry took shape gradually at the back where the kitchen had been. The end of the hall was converted into a kitchen. Naina marked out the portions that would be built into rooms. When completed, a whole house would be located behind the shop.

He got the bricks, sand, cement and hardy timber. The bricks formed a waist-high, kiln-like structure at the top of which was cemented a cauldron. A wooden ramp was constructed at one side of the cauldron, the edges resting on its lip. Three paces from this large stove rose a cement platform. Naina placed two iron drums, the insides painted, on either side. Then the work stopped. He went to Sungai Petani, then to Gurun, where there was a quarry. One evening he returned with a thrashing stone that fitted the cement dais, one end raised by a long slab of marble. Beyond the shophouse, along the dusty back lane, he planted poles and slung the twined rope for drying the clothes.

Naina began work in the shop laundry, quietly. After he had completed the day's ironing he got into his vesti, went to the back and began the boiling, thrashing and soaking of clothes. The next morning Karupi rinsed the vestis, thundus, blouses, saris, singlets and handkerchiefs that needed to be dipped in a pail of light blue dye. Part of the clothes were drying when Naina arrived. He starched the rest and hung them up on the ropes. Kumar sat out there at the back, keeping an eye on the clothes and chasing birds away.

Naina was triumphant. Menon summoned him one morning and berated him for starting a full laundry in town. He said he could have made my mother an attendant in the female wards. Menon had his responsibility to the M.O.; his workers had to strictly limit their services to the hospital.

"How can I feed all my children?" Naina said.

"Why did you have so many?" Menon said.

"Then it was that I said the words that struck the man in his face," Naina said, recounting the episode to Pather. "I won't work for you."

"I'm giving you notice," Menon said.

"No, I'm giving you notice," Naina said.

Pather chuckled. Naina rubbed his chest, smoking his cigar thoughtfully. Karupi came out to the bench with glasses of tea for the three of us.

The sundry-shop owner, three shops away, offered to put his delivery van at our disposal. Karupi, going there for the monthly provisions, had kept him informed.

My mother didn't take to the change in our fortunes. Her face was clouded the whole day. The shifting was to be done late in the evening when the long-house would be busy sitting down to its last meal. Naina he said he didn't want to flaunt his departure before Menon's eyes. Mother sorted the things and arranged them in the milk boxes Kumar and I had salvaged. I made a large box for my own things which had gathered dust and damp lying under the trestle bed. It held all my primary-school books, pencil box, the Tamil primer and the comics.

The long-house children had already gathered at our house when the truck arrived. Ganesh leaned over the window sill looking at the boxes on the floor. The lamps that had fascinated me, used frequently in the hospital house, filled a whole box. Mother had cleaned and polished them to bright, fascinating orbs and spouts.

Naina came and the loading was finished within half an hour.

"Is this all you have?" the Chinese driver said, glancing at the mats, pillows, coverlets and the boxes.

"Can we go now?" Naina said.

He helped my mother onto the bicycle carrier. I rode in the truck, beside the driver and his helper.

As the truck moved off I heard the children rush into the empty house and a noisy scramble ensued. Govindan stood in front of his house, Letchumi beside him, shouting something. It was only when the truck reached the main road that his words registered.

"Running away like thieves in the night!" he had yelled.

With the family once again under the same roof the organisation of the household and the laundry business went smoothly. The hallway between the shop and the kitchen became a conveyor belt of efforts. Karupi started the movement, sorting the clothes. Kumar marked them, the girls took them to the cauldron and the tubs. Naina thrashed them, Kumar dried them, the girls brought them back into the shop. I had more time for my books. Customers got their clothes whenever they wanted them. There was always money in the till.

One evening a brand new Austin Cambridge stopped before the shop. The driver got down and opened the back door. Menon alighted; the driver followed with a bundle of clothes.

"Is this Mynah Cleaners?" Menon said.

Naina stood as he always did before that man: hands at the sides, shoulders hunched.

"Ayah, sit down," Karupi said.

"I want these clothes washed!" Menon barked. "Bring them back in three days."

He stomped back to the car, got in, slammed the door shut and commanded the driver to move on.

When I looked at Naina I saw a fear I had never met in his eyes.

12

Naina wouldn't tolerate laziness or incompetence from anyone of us. The shop hummed the whole day. Mother attended to the cooking: vegetable curry on Tuesdays, mutton on Wednesdays and chicken on Sundays. The kettle, always on the boil, provided us with tea or coffee whenever we felt like a drink. The boys went to the cinema in Sungai Petani on Sundays, the girls to the Majestic, a hundred yards from the shophouse.

Samy was bought a Raleigh bicycle as an incentive for dedicated delivery duties. Kumar received a small transistor to while away the time as he kept watch over the clothes on the rope lines behind the laundry. The girls got whatever dresses and blouses they wanted. But they woke up at 5.30 a.m. and went to bed at 11 p.m.

I can't recall a more glorious period in our family history. We fell into the effort-reward rhythm our days imposed on us, trusting only the dreams our tired bodies allowed us. Mother was different. Though fagged out by evening she took a bath to purify herself, then lit the lamp at the shop shrine. She polished the tier lamps with ashes and *assam* and had them alight one Friday.

"Deepavali is early this year," Naina remarked.

"Who cares about customs in this place," Mother said.

---

assam – Sour substance used in curries.

"And burn up the clothes?" Naina asked.

The hall floor was littered with clothes for the wash the next morning.

"I'm going to the temple at the third mile," Mother announced on another Friday.

"Who will take you there?" Karupi said. "The children are needed here. *Hari Raya* is only a week more."

Mother didn't have her dinner that night. But these were only minor incidents. Mother soon forgot about them, packing the tier lamps, trays, and ritual vessels, in newspaper after giving them a final polish, and storing them in the large box.

"When we need them they must be there," Mother said as I watched her at work.

Amidst the talk of Independence, Naina built the two rooms across the hall in the middle of the long shophouse. The centre room was occupied by my parents, and the other one by the girls. I had my room and the boys slept up in the attic, over the shop. One night, while we were still at work on the clothes, we heard Tunku Abdul Rahman, our Prime Minister, on the radio, uttering the words: *"Merdeka! Merdeka! Merdeka!"*

So Independence came to us. Its immediate signs were the further reduction of the curfew hours and in the kind of goods displayed on the pavement stalls. From then on we had to stay indoors only between 2 and 4 a.m. But the vans that opened shop on the roadsides gave us the real sense of liberation.

The streets were filled with all kinds of hawkers, stalls, sidewalk stores, fruit carts and craftsmen. Beside the quack who pedalled lucky charms, potency beads and aphrodisiacs, stood the agent from the Chinese medicine

---

Hari Raya – Major festival of the Malays taking place immediately after the fasting month.
Merdeka – Independence.

shop, the *sin-seh*. Ginseng, roots, herbs (in large jars), and vitamin pills in handy bottles were spread out before him, on a white cloth. On the other side sat the Malay with his stock of krises, running a velvety cloth over the crooked blades. Across them the fruit stalls overflowed with oranges, pears, peaches, grapes, custard apples and apples. People bought them – they were dirt cheap – in small paper bags and munched on them as they pushed through the crowds to the various sales.

The four streets of Bedong had been sectioned off for different classes of goods. On the left, beyond the fruit stalls, were house furnishings, and these attracted the largest crowds. They trampled on each other to look, wonder-struck, at articles which had been accessible to them only in dreams. Furniture, hardy western sets, were piled up almost literally to the sky. The man had to mount an aluminium ladder to bring down a piece a customer fancied. People gave complete reign to their fantasies. Large brass bedsteads, plastic commodes and old, ornamental radio sets and grams were carted off in tricycles. Women picked well-used plastic tubs, apparently coming from colonial bungalows, for bathing children in, and filled them with cutlery, soap dishes, frying pans and dessert spoons. One Indian bought an electric oven with compartments, thinking it was a chic clothes cupboard!

Kumar bought a plastic rack for toothbrushes, Naina a whole range of wooden hangers with grips to them. I grabbed an antique silver phone, the head-and-mouthpiece mounted on a box-like stand. These street sales went on for days. The mat-seller, the potter and the snake charmer were lonely figures, attracting one or two restless onlookers. I saw a whole world rise beside the road, cramped and glittering, towards the reachable peaks of personal dreams. Possession

---

sin-seh – Chinese folk medical expert.

wasn't exclusive any more: it was everyone's prerogative.

Menon changed his car once more, this time to a Mercedes. He stopped off at our shop, unloading a whole batch of suits and dainty handkerchiefs. His son, dressed in Terylene trousers and an Arrow shirt, watched, standing beside the car. Mrs. Menon talked, briefly, to Karupi, without alighting from the car. Menon looked briefly at me, then turned to Naina.

"You're still washing my clothes!" he said, a vengeful gleam in his eyes.

Naina looked him in the face, then gestured to me. I wrote out a receipt for Menon's clothes at the formica counter.

"Each man makes his way in life as best as he can," Naina said in Tamil, handing the receipt to Menon.

The limp gave Menon a click at his heels as he walked back to the Mercedes.

"Why do you accept his clothes?" I asked Naina.

"He pays like any one else," he said.

PERIATHAI was dying of cancer. Kumar visited her in the mornings; I went to her in the evenings. Naina came away from her late in the night. Periathai wouldn't leave her house or the land on which it stood. The town knew of her tussle with the Town Council.

"Buy the land for her," many advised Naina.

"I've asked. It isn't for sale," Naina said morosely.

From various parts of the country came Periathai's sons, their wives and grandchildren. Except for Naina, her sons had lost themselves in the estates and townlets in Malaysia. Velu, her eldest son, was the first to go away to seek his fortune. Sometimes Naina received a letter from Batu Pahat, in Johor. My uncle, Velu, was doing all right; his sons were helping him run the sundry shop in a kampung, a few miles from the town. Raju, my younger uncle, worked in the army base in Kuala Lumpur and lived with his family in Sentul, near the fringe of the city centre.

Naina sent telegrams the week Periathai was critically silent. Her descendants came, clutching suitcases and paperbags. The men wore the latest in shirts and shoes, their women the most fashionable in the sari range. The children, turned out in mini-suits and fluffy, ready-made dresses, paraded before Periathai. They came prepared to camp out Periathai's death.

Tents were pitched in the ruined kolam compound. The women and children slept under one, cooking and feeding in Periathai's kitchen. Naina bore the expenses, being the son near whom Periathai had chosen to stay. The men trooped to the town in the mornings, sat around in coffeeshops, and in the evenings surreptitiously drank in the toddy shop. They came back cheerful and talkative, bathed, had their dinner and played "troupe" with the potter, barbers, sextons, drummers and Periathai's many customers, in the other tent.

Bedong had long been a "white area" when Periathai died that morning, her eyes still gazing at us. The usual funeral preparations didn't begin at once. The men continued playing cards, the children feeding in the kitchen. Only the women wailed, Uncle Velu's wife the loudest, because it was Indian custom. My other grandmother, impatient at the delay, washed, with the help of some other women, and laid out Periathai in her best sari.

The drummers built a crackling fire out of dry, coconut-tree leaves, warmed their drums, and the first rhythms announced Periathai's death to Bedong. But some man, coming out of the death room, stopped them. The older women protested.

"Can't she go peacefully to her grave?"

The men had returned, primed with toddy and samsu,

Uncle Velu talking rapidly and gesturing. Uncle Raju, at the
fringe of the men who had gathered around Uncle Velu,
kept protesting. They stopped abruptly when they saw
Naina come into the compound. Uncle Velu drank quickly
from a flat bottle and came up to Naina.

"I want to talk to you," he said aggressively.

Just then one of the drummers approached Naina.

"Did you give orders for the drumming to be stopped?"

"I don't have four pairs of ears," Naina said. "Come to
the tent and we'll talk calmly."

"We've been talking the whole day. The body is
rotting!" Uncle Velu said.

"Don't talk with disrespect about our mother," Naina
said.

"You're the one being disrespectful. Letting her lie
there the whole day!" Uncle Velu said.

"She must be given a good burial," Naina said, angrily.
"What have you done as her sons?"

"I've a family to look after," Uncle Raju said quickly.

"Who hasn't a family? Coming here, dressed up like
that, as if for Deepavali," Naina said.

"You can't put her away quietly," the drummer said.
"Almost everyone in Bedong knows her."

"An outsider has more feeling," Naina said.

"It's all right for him. For the next three days he can
eat and sleep here. And gulp down toddy by the gallon,"
Uncle Velu said.

"Toddy or no toddy, he has more affection for our
mother than you," Naina said.

"What do you want us to do?" Uncle Raju said. "Die
with her?"

"Wait until she's properly under the ground, and then
crawl back to your holes," Naina said.

The older Indian women of Bedong, who had
knowledge of embalming techniques, worked on Periathai.

They padded her up, restored the face so that she looked as if she had come back from a wedding. Her arms were plastered with sandalwood paste, but her wrinkled wrists showed through the numerous bangles. Naina was satisfied. The drumming went on in the compound, visitors filed in. The wake had begun. It had gone into the third day when another quarrel flared up.

"What's the matter with you, Kannan?" Uncle Velu shouted. "Don't you want her in the ground? Don't you want us to go home?"

"There's no hurry," Naina said, indifferently.

He hadn't changed his clothes since the day Periathai died and he had lost weight. His matted hair fell over bloodshot eyes. He had been drinking steadily, but looked only as if he had just got up from bed.

"People have paid their respects. Now we've got to start the ceremonies," Uncle Raju said.

"There are still people who haven't seen her for the last time," Naina said.

Karupi came out of Periathai's room. She had aged, her eyes ready to close with sleep.

"The women can't stay there too long," she said.

Naina grasped an old butt of a coconut leaf and beat her, mechanically, Karupi unprotesting. My two uncles rushed towards Naina and restrained him. Naina sat at a table, slumped over and cried. Uncle Velu stood near him, occasionally placing his hand on Naina's shoulder.

"She had to go, as all have to go," Uncle Velu said.

Naina raised his head, a fierce expression on his face. His tears had dried.

"That woman I took as my wife out of charity, says my mother stinks!" he suddenly shouted.

"We're all tired and can't control our thoughts," Uncle Velu said.

"The months she had you in her belly! And you can't

wait for a few days," Naina said.

Naina's shoulders shook again, and he blubbered. The women signalled to my two uncles. They waited until Naina emerged from the tremor of grief. But before anyone could stop him, Naina had gone to the coconut-leaf bathshed, bathed, returned and put on a change of clothes. He stood once more before the mumbling, protesting relatives and mourners.

"This isn't done," said the priest who had been hired to officiate at the complicated funeral rites. "You take your bath only *after* she has been buried."

"Where's your backbone?" Naina said, "She didn't respect worm-eaten customs, she changed them!"

"We must have customs, Kannan," the priest argued. "That's something bigger than man's fault-making thoughts."

"My mother will receive the grandest funeral," Naina said. "I've the money. So do what you're told."

Then he was gone. When he reappeared, Bayi, attentive and smiling, was with him. Naina took out a wad of notes and distributed them among the chief drummer, sexton, the priest and Uncle Velu.

"The funeral is tomorrow. We cremate her," Naina said. "The whole of Bedong will know that Periathai died the way she lived."

Uncle Velu was put in charge of the post-funeral feast. Though the priest prohibited meat, Naina wouldn't listen. The important people of Bedong had to be feted, he said. Just as these arrangements were being discussed a small bus arrived. White-uniformed men alighted with their brass instruments.

"The band will play for my mother," Naina said to an astonished crowd.

The musicians occupied a tent, set up their scores and, sitting on chairs they had brought, played the opening bars of a solemn, maudlin tune. From then on the funeral became a dramatic, glamorous event, punctuated by quarrels and Naina's angry shouts. The crowds came again, attracted by the band's music and the drummers' angry beats.

The hearse arrived the following morning. Naina had worked out a route for the procession: it would go in the opposite direction, towards the junction, head for the laundry shop, turn and complete the march through the town, and then return to the laterite road to get to the Indian cemetery. The procession started in the afternoon and took nearly two hours to circle the town, and, finally, come to a standstill at the pyre built on the edge of the cemetery.

The sons and grandsons, after completing the rites at the pyre, were driven back in cars to the shop. Cooking had begun three hours before; we bathed and, putting on the simplest clothes, awaited the guests. Tables were laid in the shop proper, the hall behind it, and even in the two, newly-built rooms. An endless stream of sympathisers arrived, ate noisily at the tables, munched sireh on the benches outside the shop, and departed. Then the Mercedes stopped at the shop; Naina rushed forward, welcomed Menon, and accompanied him to a table covered with a white cloth. Some of the hospital staff who had been waiting, sat down with Menon. So did Bayi. Beer was served.

The town talked of nothing but the funeral procession and the feasting and Naina's grief for a whole week. At unexpected moments, even away from the shop, he burst into tears. People looked away as the hysterical sobbing shook his weak and lean body. When he resumed work in the laundry he still wore mourning clothes, but by that time customers had begun calling for their clothes.

Karupi ruled with an iron hand. Even when Naina was caught by an unexpected bout of grief, he had to quickly wipe his eyes and continue thrashing at the stone. If Karupi hadn't been there we would have been lost. She knew how to talk to impatient customers, my over-worked brothers and sisters, and even my mother. Naina had incurred heavy debts over the funeral expenses; Bayi became, once more, a familiar sight in the shop. Sometimes Mrs. Menon summoned Karupi summarily. She dropped whatever she was doing and hurried to the hospital bungalow.

Naina worked stolidly. I heard him late in the laundry, humming a melancholy tune. But he was up early and at the ironing table. Mother cooked whatever Karupi bought, at her own discretion, in the market. It was a few months before we had chicken for our meals. I thanked myself for having obtained the scholarship; Naina was up to his neck in debt. Menon grinned triumphantly at me if he happened to pass me in his car.

Periathai's accumulation of kitchen ware and ritual articles were brought to the shop in her tin trunks. Naina looked at them for a while, his eyes clouding, then told my mother to store them. Periathai's trunks stood beside our own boxes in our parents' room. Naina gave strict orders that the lamps, long-necked vessels and Nataraja weren't ever to be taken out of the trunks.

13

A year after Periathai's death, Naina had settled most of the minor debts. I was in Form Four, well past my adolescence and, having read some English novels, I began to understand the simple mechanism, I thought, of the Malaysian Indian. I recognised the spirit that had touched Periathai and now possessed Naina. He continued the battle Periathai had begun: to drive some stake into the country. The restlessness that had motivated Periathai into building her houses and keeping the kolam courtyard decorated, meaningful, and intact, took another form in my father. More complex than Karupi, the intensity with which he turned Periathai's funeral into a show, had frightened me. I stood outside Periathai's and Naina's preoccupations. Their imagination couldn't grasp the real complexity that surrounded us. I had, watching Periathai's failure to earn a home in this land, decided to acquire a skill that would allow me a comfortable, unthreatened existence. One's world was, after all, private, and it was only through chance encounters, as had been Miss Nancy's and mine, that one discovered the logic and the power that sustains the individual. A mild anger filled me as I saw Periathai die homeless. But I considered hers an irrational attitude. No one would compel me into sharing another, immature ambition.

Only my studies mattered. I was at them constantly,

aware that I could go to England if I won a teaching bursary. Naina's interests and my family's struggles became unimportant. The dignity of the individual was the only thing that engaged me. And this couldn't be acquired if I gave in to quirkish desires and irrational dreams. My father had surrendered to some secret grief at Periathai's death and borrowed indiscriminately to salve a non-existent pride. He had to pay for his impulsive behaviour.

It was amusing to watch the family repair its broken image. Naina drove himself relentlessly. Bayi kept coming and Menon's wife summoning Karupi.

"Have you the hundred for Bayi this month?" Karupi asked.

"Give him just the interest. As long as he gets his beer he won't insist," Naina said.

"We'll have to reduce household expenses," Karupi said.

Naina was silent for a while; Mother worked assiduously in the kitchen. She didn't participate in the family councils which were mainly financial in nature. Naina drew figures on the floor of the hall, reflectively.

"The girls have to be married off," he said, interrupting his calculations on the imaginary slate before him. "We don't want this town to spit on us again."

"But we've so many debts to settle," Karupi said. "How can we work harder? We don't even rest any more."

"We've worked to the bone before. We can do it again," Naina said. "We've got to increase our income."

The old wheel ground through its circle. Naina and Karupi brooded while Mother went on placidly bending over the stoves. Once more she attempted to light the tier lamps and Naina nearly thrashed her.

"What's the good of wasting oil!" he shouted. "Can't you see under the electric light?"

"We don't even light the oil lamp at the shop shrine,"

Mother said. "Must everything have a use?"

"I'll knock your teeth in if you don't go back to the kitchen," Naina said.

Mother mumbled something about a godless house; Naina caught her by the hair and Karupi had to come in between.

"The girls will start crying. Tomorrow's wash will be delayed," she said.

The family talked, plotted and worked outside my door. I did my share in the afternoons, at the formica counter. I would soon be in Form Five, the School Certificate Examination round the corner. The door of my room remained closed except for those brief hours in the afternoons. But the planning and the quarrels filtered through, an interfering vibration to my scholarly tasks.

"Why did you let your brothers have your mother's jewelry and money?" Karupi said. "At this time they could have been pawned."

"We can always accumulate property," Naina said. "Those brothers of mine are showy loafers. They want the easy way out."

"Who will marry you if you can't cook?" Mother said to my sister. "I go to the bathroom and come back and the dhal is singed!"

"I'm busy helping them," my sister said. "They need me more."

"Your future husband won't eat clothes," Mother said.

"Just mention marriage and you make it a Ramayana," Naina said.

I shut off the conversation, turning more seriously to my work and only the light, burning late into the night out in the hall, irritated me. The boys, Samy and Kumar, fought playfully up in the attic, relieved at last from work.

"Can't you see I'm trying to sleep!" I shouted at them. "I've got school tomorrow."

"We don't get time to play during the day!" Kumar said.

The year turned as my family renewed its efforts against insolvency. Samy and Kumar, like me, had become sober. Kumar took on my duties at the counter; he had picked up the rudiments of receipt-writing and clothes-shelving. Ingenious and diligent, he rigged up a tin clapper to shoo away the birds at the back, manipulating it with a string from the shop front. Though younger than me by three years, he looked more an adult. His hard, angular face possessed Naina's quiet strength. Sometimes he came into my room without knocking on the door, and sat on the bed watching me.

The town had forgiven Naina that week of unpredictable behaviour during Periathai's funeral. Bayi stood more humbly at the counter when he came for his money. Provision-shop proprietors vied with each other for Naina's custom. He was trusted and respected; he seemed to rise superbly out of each financial crisis. The talk became less strained outside my door. One night Naina was talkative. He unfolded his scheme to raise capital for two more shops, one in Merbok and the other in Gurun.

Naina began to go out from the shop more often. After a month, strange men appeared at our doorstep, Chinese and Indians who rode up in cars. They had a brisk air about them and I was sent for beers. While I stood ironing, resentful, Naina talked with them. In the evening he got into their car and went away, to return late at night, tipsy and full of plans. He made me write out receipts in a booklet he had specially printed, for a thousand dollars. I made out sixteen.

Karupi, Samy and Kumar accompanied Naina to Merbok and Gurun, to inspect prospective shops. These excursions affected business in the shop.

"We'll get them back and more," Naina said, a certain dream in his eyes.

He knocked on my door one night.

"Don't shut yourself up all the time," he said. "Show some interest in what we're doing for the family."

Karupi, Samy and Kumar were seated at the table bought only that week. They looked excited and determined.

"Sit down, Ravi," Karupi said.

I sat on a new chair Kumar pushed towards me. Naina sat down at the head.

"You have to sit for the final examination this year," Naina said. "But we too have been going through some tests."

Samy giggled at the parallel.

"Now we must all work together," Naina continued. "We've, up to now, worked for others. It's time we thought of ourselves."

"We're opening shops in Merbok and Gurun," Karupi cut in impatiently. "We need people to manage them."

"I can only help a little," I said. "This examination is too important."

"What's more important than building our own house? Examinations all the time!" Naina said angrily. "Your grandmother died without a house to her name."

"Don't scold him. He knows things," Karupi said. "What am I saying? He's almost a man!"

"You think reading English books is enough in life!" Naina said and paused for a while.

"Can you run the shop in Gurun?" he asked.

I shook my head.

"Boys from Gurun go to your school in Sungai Petani," Karupi said. "You won't be late for lessons."

The thought of leaving my room upset me. I worked best there and it harboured my dreams and image. Shifting at that time of the year, getting accustomed to a new place and people, and travelling a longer distance to school would throw me out of gear.

I shook my head again.

"What can you do then?" Naina demanded angrily.

"I'll look after the Gurun shop, Naina," Kumar volunteered.

"I want to know what your brother, Ravi, is good for," Naina persisted.

"I'll manage this shop," I said.

"He can do that. He's still helping," Karupi said.

The matter was settled. Karupi would rule the Merbok shop, Kumar in Gurun and I would remain in the Bedong "Mynah Cleaners". I resented the heavier responsibility, but that was the only thing I could do to placate Naina. We had an amicable and large meal that night. I was informed that Menon and Bayi had been paid off. Naina had twelve thousand dollars from the pool he had organised with sixteen people, he having paid four shares.

The Merbok and Gurun branches went into operation almost immediately. Naina kept shuttling between the three shops, supervising the few men he had employed to wash and iron. I read more at the counter than in my room, keeping an eye on Ramasamy who did the pressing. I had to be particularly careful in the evenings when the toddy shop opened. He was liable to disappear for a few hours then.

Mother kept to herself, lighting the tier lamps on the nights Naina slept in Merbok or Gurun.

In October that year, when I lived under the examination fever daze, Naina bought a second-hand Morris. He had never held a driving license and so employed a driver. Samy washed the Morris whenever it came back, dusty, from its many trips to Merbok and Gurun. Work went on at a fast pace in the Bedong shop though Naina rarely stood behind the thrashing stone.

I sat for the School Certificate Examination and passed well. While waiting for the selections for the teacher-training

course in England to be announced, I visited the shops in
Merbok and Gurun. They were showier than I had
expected. The showcases were entirely glass, the wrapping
paper colourful and shiny. In each a radio was tuned on the
whole day. Kumar in Gurun brought in more returns than
Karupi in Merbok, the competition keeping them
quarrelsome and hardworking. Naina was like the white
M.O. who appeared only on occasional visits. How he spent
the rest of the time, mystified me.

Before I was due to fly to England, having been
selected from thousands of candidates, I attended my sister's
wedding. Mother cried and insisted I go through an entire
departure ritual, starting with a fast, then a bath, and finally
a prolonged kneeling at the shrine she had improvised in
the hall.

"I don't know when I'll place this holy line on your
forehead again," she said, sobbing.

I took the day train to Kuala Lumpur, and although I
spent the night before the flight alone, in a hotel room, I
was relieved.

14

The two years in England passed quickly. The snow wasn't as white as I had imagined it to be: it muddied the moment the flakes touched the ground. The sky was almost always clouded. But these didn't diminish the pleasure of my stay. Miss Nancy's landscape lingered in my mind, seeing me through the bleak, dark winter. And Ernie appeared among the many faces I saw in that midland town or in London.

The cleaner, waiting outside the toilet to swab up, at first awed me, but soon I took him as part of English life. I got along well with the lecturers, the gardeners who kept the many flower beds on the college grounds trim, the women cleaners and the van driver. I visited, at last, Wordsworth's cottage, tramped through the Lake District with pride of possession and the passion of the elite. But my final triumph came when I taught English children, during teaching practice, in Monkmoor Secondary School near Lawrence's collier country.

My impression of England is summed up in my encounter with Judith Crawfurd during my last teaching practice, in Monkmoor. Miss Crawfurd – she never allowed me to refer to her by her Christian name – was a firm, devoted teacher. Her sharp blue eyes, mounted on a very fair, dry face, bored directly into you, assessing and slotting you. Somehow the effort to win Miss Crawfurd's approval became more important than obtaining the best grades from my lecturers. Miss Crawfurd didn't give over her classes to me, as the other teachers did, thankful for the free periods I provided. Instead, she sat, hawk-eyed, lesson after lesson, at the back of the class, until I approached something like her efficiency.

"My classes are safe with you," she said one morning and glided off to the library.

The hours I spent in her classes were informative and exciting. At first, after Miss Crawfurd's disappearance, the students gave reign to mischief. They would interrupt me in the middle of the lesson to ask a facile question or to have the windows (it was late autumn), closed. If they were given grammar exercises, they rushed for pens, pencils, rulers and erasers at my desk, a particularly high one with a heavy lid. But having learnt from Miss Crawfurd's methods, I screwed them down firmly to their seats. I distributed everything, fairly, at the beginning of each lesson.

"Do you have everything now?" I said, and paused. "If you don't you have only yourselves to blame!"

After the first week with them I was accepted by all except one shy, reticent boy. He never spoke in my classes but produced studied, excellent essays. The other boys and girls would look, suppressing giggles, in his direction if I pointedly asked him a question. But Allan never said a word, not even during the reading and dramatisation of *Tom Brown's Schooldays*, until I set the class an essay on death.

"Do you think people go to heaven when they die, Sir?" he asked, the words coming in a rush.

"Perhaps they do," I said.

I read through their simple ideas about death, but Allan's essay made me sit up. I learned of his attachment to his father, how his father had died in a car accident, and of Allan's grief. The boy's sorrow was unashamed and genuine. After handing in the work he disappeared from class. Miss

Crawfurd came after me.

"What did you do to Allan?" she said.

"Nothing."

"Why didn't you report his absence?"

"He may have reasons for staying away," I said.

"He has. His father died recently. He withdrew from everything. You've destroyed months of patient work, bringing him out of himself."

"What are you accusing me of?" I asked.

"Of overlooking the fact that he's a special boy. Of bad teaching methods. Didn't you offer an alternative topic?" she said.

"I did," I lied.

Allan turned up three days later; he spoke more often in class, submitted sensitive essays and joined in the dramatisation of *Tom Brown's Schooldays*. Miss Crawfurd came into the staff-room one morning and offered me a cup of tea, a rare gesture, I was told, from her.

"You've cured Allan of his melancholy, Mr. Ravi," she said.

The month at Monkmoor ended too swiftly for me. I walked away from the modest tea party in my honour, completely confident of myself. The children in their overcoats and mufflers rushed about the playground. A boy came towards me from the isolated wing of the unpainted library. It was Allan. I extended my hand but he didn't take it.

"You lied about the essay," he said, and stood there looking at me.

I walked away thinking that the boy was still touched by his father's death, Miss Crawfurd's smile of acceptance in my mind.

The letters from home were few but the addresses had changed several times. Kumar, who had kept up that trickle of correspondence, wrote of strange changes in Naina. I decided on the shop address in Bedong for the box of books I had accumulated, to be sent by boat. With a lot of misgivings, I packed my suitcase, which, being a light traveller, I hadn't touched for two years, and the hand bag. I stared at the flashing English countryside from the coach taking me to the airport in London, vowing I would return one day.

A different, grim, set of scenes accompanied me as I took the night mail from Kuala Lumpur to Bukit Mertajam, after the plane touched down. Kuala Lumpur Railway Station, in contrast to Piccadilly Circus or Victoria, was stifling, ill-lit, and smelly. A row of wagons stood on the tracks, ready to cart us into a dark nowhere. As the train clacked past, I caught glimpses of squatter huts, clumps of banana trees, a man bathing — a kerosine lamp flickering — beside a well. Then for half an hour the train ground through a bizarre, moonlit patch of jungle. But by then I had slumped into my seat behind a rank latrine, the excitement of coming home evaporated.

Then suddenly the morning light revealed an old, overhead railway bridge, a huddle of shophouses and tin sheds. I had arrived at Bukit Mertajam. No one was waiting for me, although I had only expected Kumar. My ears still singing from the flight, I took a taxi, after a long discussion with the driver, to Sungai Petani, and from there another to the Bedong shop.

It was strangely empty, the plywood wall separating Pather and the showcases torn down. The man, grayed and even drier, hunched over the work desk. Karupi came running to meet me, throwing her thavani over her shoulder, crying. She held on to my suitcase, then left it and darted into the back. Her sons, my half-brothers, had grown during those two years. But they showed only a flicker of recognition in their eyes. Karupi hurriedly returned with a tray of saffron water, burning camphor cubes floating in the middle.

"You arrived so suddenly," she said.

She waved the tray thrice over my head and threw the contents on the road. Mother would have broken a coconut as well. I feared the worst, seeing only my half-brothers and half-sisters gazing, unconcerned, at me. The shop had lost its liveliness and glamour. The rattan chairs had come untwined, the arms completely bare with nail heads sticking out. The showcases were only half-filled, sooty and cobwebbed in the corners. The formica counter had peeled.

"Sit down, Ravi, my son," she said gushingly.

I sat down in one of the derelict, rattan chairs, my ears buzzing, my eyes hurt by the bright sunlight. Karupi reappeared with a glass of tea.

"They are preparing your old room," she said.

The boys stood looking at me as if they barely believed I existed. Then I was overcome by fatigue, and, hardly noticing the changes in the room, entered a deep sleep. I only got up for meals during the following two days. On the third I was wide awake, desolate and miserable. The room was dark and dingy; pictures of glamorous Indian film actresses had replaced my posters. The bedstead creaked, the mattress become lumpy. The cupboard, though still locked, with my books and letters inside, was scratched all over. The ornate desk had lost its lid.

Just then I heard a commotion in the shop, and Naina's voice came through.

"Naina," I said, hiding my surprise.

He wore a white vesti and a crumpled but clean shirt. His hair was cropped short and had grayed. The face, harder, looked moulded by a new dream. His eyes, sunk deep now, gazed at me solemnly.

"I waited a long time for you," he said. "Thank God you're back."

He took and held my hand for a few minutes. His eyes

moistened and he looked like a small child, ill-treated and lost.

"Yes, I've come back," I said, trying to give him strength.

"Have you rested?" he said. "I gave them orders not to disturb you. You've flown in an aeroplane and you've lived among strange people. But you've returned."

He sat on the bed, fidgetting for a while, then, going back to an old habit, rubbed his chest. For a moment he was the man I had known, sober and determined. He got up abruptly.

"Your mother is preparing a home-coming meal," he said. "Kumar will show you the house."

After he had gone, Kumar entered the room and stood beside the bed, silent and unsure. Then he began to cry, Karupi watching impassively from the doorway.

"He has given up everything," Kumar said, still sobbing. "He wants to build a house near the river."

"No one chased him away," Karupi said. "Ravi, he borrowed money everywhere. The *kootu* people wanted their money back. I've been paying back some people."

"You made him open all those shops," Kumar said, hate in his eyes. "When business was bad, you still wanted to keep them open."

"Don't put your father's mistakes on my head," Karupi said. "This is how they talk nowadays. If I didn't show them the way, they would have starved. Be careful, Ravi. They want to turn you against me."

"Come and see Mother," Kumar said. "I'll wait outside."

I followed him, after a bath and change of clothes, past the row of sundry goods shops, the deserted railway station. We took the *lallang*-fringed path between the

---

kootu – A monthly pool, won by bidding.
lallang – Malaysian tall, wild grass.

railway tracks and the main road. A small hut rose in a bit of cleared land, about twenty yards from the river.

"That's our house now," Kumar said. "Naina wants to build it bigger."

In my absence, the family had split. They must have acquired, I thought, the quarrelsome spirit from having lived in the long-house. It was sad that Naina had abandoned work, comfort and security for a hut almost at the fringe of the jungle. We crossed the road and trod the mud track, criss-crossed by bicycle tyre marks, to the hut. My mother put me through a complete welcoming ceremony.

It was more than a hut, I found, on closer inspection. There were two rooms, a hall and a kitchen. Naina sat in one room where Periathai's silver and copper lamps, the Nataraja statue and a statuette of *Saraswathi* had been set up. The light showed Naina in deep contemplation. A broad thurnuru mark covered his forehead. I was in the kitchen, teasing my youngest brother, about five years old, when Naina emerged from his room.

"Are you surprised?" he said.

"Things have changed," I said.

"This is a nice piece of land. The river isn't too far away," he said. "Have you seen the well?"

"He has just come back from another country," Mother said. "Give him time to understand what you're doing."

"He'll understand. He went to the white man's country to study," Naina said with deep conviction.

The meal was a feast: we sat in a circle and ate from banana leaves. The chicken curry had a lingering taste. Vegetables, with hardly any spices, were wholesome and fragrant.

"We grow them ourselves," Naina said simply.

Kumar's battery transistor was turned on softly, after

Saraswathi – Hindu Goddess of Learning.

the family had gone to sleep. I lay on a thin mattress in the hall, near a window open to the night air. Kumar had fetched my clothes and some books from the shop.

In the morning I got a full view of the land. Naina, up before sunrise, had worked on the furrows beyond the well, a few yards from the house. Chillie plants, long beans, lady's fingers and other vegetables grew abundantly. The air smelled of manure, turned earth and plants in flower.

Naina talked to me most evenings, mainly about the extensions to the house he had in mind, fencing the land and buying cattle. I listened, waiting for my appointment letter, and wishing to get away again.

"If we don't build this house together it isn't a house," Naina said.

Kumar worked in a petrol kiosk and gave his entire pay to my mother. Samy, a factory hand in Sungai Petani, surrendered as much as he could spare. Naina expected me to contribute the largest share towards fulfilling his dreams. The life was simple, the household expenses manageable, but I was disappointed with Naina's ambition.

Finally the appointment letter came. Though I had asked for a town in Perak, I was posted to a new secondary school in Sungai Petani.

15

After the initial month in the new school, my life fell into a pattern. The day started with work; I corrected exercises before I left for school. At first I walked from the room I rented to the school, less than a mile away. Then I acquired a motorcycle. After the last bell, I joined the single, men teachers at a Chinese stall for lunch. After an afternoon nap, I was ready for badminton at the Sungai Petani Club courts. Then, with the sweat still on our bodies, we drank tall glasses of Coke or fresh orange. After dinner, I went back to my books. Some weekends the teachers organised parties where I drank a glass of beer. There were few departures from this routine: occasionally I went to Penang to catch a film that would take months to reach the Sungai Petani cinemas. If I was restless some nights, after the lessons had been prepared and books marked, I attributed it to the demands of a teaching job.

My visits to the house by the river, in Bedong, were regular and brief. On the last trip, at the end of the month, I handed whatever money I could spare. It was more than Kumar and Samy together gave. I only pretended to listen if Kumar talked family politics. I wasn't interested in why business had failed and Naina had turned to the land. My own wish was to keep out of whatever mess they might create. At first, distance helped.

Naina, determined to carry out his plans, had ordered

more planks, sand and cement. They were piled up beside the house. Naina pointed out the sites of the additional rooms, walking proudly over them as if they already existed. He rambled on in Tamil while I listened impatiently, waiting for the meal Mother was preparing. Mother insisted I eat a full dinner whenever I visited the family. I couldn't leave with her reproachful face thrust out at me.

"You have to help your father," she told me when I stayed longer than usual. "Why don't the others understand him? He put his hand to everything. When you were in England, he came home with so much money. But his fate wasn't good."

"You can't do anything without money!" I said. "How is he going to build this into a larger house?"

"He can make the money. But he says the whole family must help," she said. "Karupi likes living in town. To him the river is the most important thing."

Once again I was forced merely to listen. Why did my mother sympathise with Naina's backward dreams? He was afraid of a competitive world, where you are always tested, as I was.

The planks lay warped, the sand hardened, beside the house, while Naina sat more often in the shrine-room. If I made a hasty visit on a weekend morning, I saw my mother polishing the tier lamps and the other copper vessels with assam and ash. She was happy, the house lighted up on Friday evenings. She tried forming the kolams within the house but her fingers were stiff.

"We don't need kolams any more," she said. "Otherwise they would come."

She didn't believe in the disciplined acquisition of a skill. They had to "come" or they were unimportant.

"I need more money," Naina told me on another visit.

"I'm giving all I can," I said.

"Not enough. The eldest son must give more," he said.

From that evening my visits to the house became less frequent. My mother grumbled.

"After telling you all I did, you still behave like this," she said.

"You said Naina doesn't need money. But he's asking for it all the time," I said.

"You can give him more," she said calmly.

"I need money to live," I said.

"Buying books and records all the time. Kumar told me," she said.

"You can't sit doing nothing in a room all day," I said.

"You can come here."

"There's nothing here."

Kumar worked double shifts. During the day he was a lorry attendant and in the evenings he manned the petrol pumps at the junction. He turned up suddenly at my rented room on the days the lorry passed the road near which I lived.

"You've got to come home often," he said, standing respectfully near my table. "Naina respects you more than anyone else."

"Because I'm the only one who has a good job?" I said.

"No," he said. "If you don't come for two weeks his ways change. He goes to town to drink."

"If you don't work, that's what you do," I said cuttingly.

"But you come, Brother," he said and left.

Samy rode up with a friend on a motorcycle late one night. He looked anxious.

"Come home quickly, Brother, Mother wants you," he said.

"This is what happens when I stay too near you all," I said.

"You've got to come," Samy said. "We can't control Naina any more."

When I reached a silent house, Mother came to me, her finger on her lips.

"He's sleeping," she said.

"I was doing the same thing," I said, irritated.

"He talked about you the whole evening, then got drunk and started breaking things in the kitchen."

"I don't know why he should be angry," I said.

"Men wearing government clothes came around the house," Mother said.

"You can't stay on this land," I said. "They will chase you away."

"Where can we go?" Mother said anxiously. "Can't we buy this land?"

"It isn't for sale," I said. "Some government land can't be bought."

It was history repeating itself: Periathai had somehow been perceptive in her last words. Her spirit really roamed the land, houseless! Why couldn't Naina accept that fact? At least Periathai had made, even if deluded, a fair compromise. She had accepted a temporary tenure.

Naina worked with frenzy for the next three months. Whenever I came to the house, I found it changed. It was roomy now, with a complete kitchen and two more rooms. Samy and Kumar had a room each.

"Stay with us now," Mother said. "We've got many rooms."

"There's no electric light. I don't like to live on borrowed land," I said.

"Look at the houses on the other side of the river," Naina said. "The people there are not disturbed."

"They were here long before we came," I said.

"Then we'll stay as long," Naina said.

"They are used to living off the land," I said.

"You're an educated boy," Naina said. "Can't you see? We can make all the money, get all the learning. But these are useless if our house pillars don't sink into the clay of the land."

I increased my remittance to the family, made the trip to the ungainly house as often as I could. Naina had driven poles, trimmed and shaped out of jungle trees, into the ground. Along them he nailed thinner branches so that a fence enclosed the land. He began systematically, crouching morning and afternoon over the land, to weed out the lallang. After a couple of months the house and its large patch of cultivated fields rose like a dream beside the main road. There were often bags of groundnuts, boxes of papayas, whole batches of chillies, standing in the kitchen.

Then the notice of eviction came from the Town Council.

"Notice to move," I said even as I opened the brown envelope.

"Read it to me," Naina said, smiling.

I read the formal communication.

Naina smiled again as he placed the envelope at the foot of Nataraja, in the shrine-room.

"They can't shake us," he said.

I went back to Sungai Petani, sceptical. The look on his face had frightened me, taken me back to Periathai's funeral. He had the same, obsessed stare in his eyes.

We, Samy and I, went one morning to claim Kumar's body from the Alor Setar General Hospital mortuary. The lorry he had been working on had skidded, turned, and pinned him beneath. His body was crushed, waist downwards. Naina didn't cry when he received the news. Instead he prepared the house to receive Kumar's body. We carried the corpse on a stretcher from a lorry, down the well-trodden path, to the house. In the shrine-room Naina had improvised a wooden platform.

Naina ordered the women to wash Kumar, dress him in his Deepavali clothes, and lay him out on the dais. He had incense smoking and camphor burning in a mound. He sat cross-legged before Kumar's covered body, a large *pottu* on my dead brother's face. I watched Naina sprinkle more incense and break another packet of camphor. From time to time he gazed at Nataraja across my brother's body.

Outside the house people had begun to gather. The drummers who had come to Periathai's funeral were assembled again over a fire. The leader recognised me and beckoned.

"We've come to do free service. Your father never forgot us when he had money," he said.

Govindan stood among the hospital attendants, talking in a toddy-sated drawl. He nodded to me, his speech blurred and loud.

" 'Kannan,' I said," he drawled, " 'why not return to the hospital? The Ayah will always take you back. He knows you're sorry.' "

I passed on to the kitchen. Mother sat slumped in a corner, away from the pots. Her face contorted with grief when she saw me.

"My sons are leaving me one by one," she said.

"It was an accident, Mother," I said.

"He needn't have worked so hard," she said.

Though the women wailed the whole afternoon and drummers warmed the hides and beat out the eternal story of arrival and departure, Naina sat on in the shrine-room. The crowd shuffled about restlessly. Some men had begun a card game in the hall. The women, in between simulated whining, gossiped. Towards evening the men complained loudly.

"We didn't come here to while away the time," one said.

"Is Kannan a father? The poor, crushed boy must be

---

pottu – Dot on the forehead.

buried quickly," said another.

The sexton, who had been squatting near the drummers, spoke up, drunk and confused.

"No one told me anything about a grave."

Naina emerged from the house looking determined.

"You can dig a grave in the corner of this land," he said.

The men protested.

"Bury him in a proper graveyard."

"What's the difference between the living and the dead?" Naina said.

"It isn't done."

"I don't want to hide him. He must be buried on this land," Naina said.

"You're breaking the law," Muthiah, the dispenser, said.

"I'm ready to go to jail," Naina said. "If you don't want to dig the grave, say so. I'll do it myself."

"Not that, Kannan," Govindan said.

"What? You're all cowards. Hiding behind people, women's saris and money," Naina shouted. "You're not alive and you're not dead! What are you? You've no dreams!"

He ran round to the back of the house where the *changkuls* were kept, and grabbed one. The men forced the changkul out of his hand.

"I'll dig the grave, Ayah," the sexton said. "Can't let a father dig his own son's grave."

The men and women chattered excitedly among themselves. I looked away when one of them pointed to his head and rolled his eyes.

"He always likes to make a show," a woman said. "Why can't he live and die quietly like others?"

"Shut your mouth, woman!" my mother shouted.

---

changkul – Malaysian hoe.

The men trooped towards the edge of the land, beside the fence. The changkuls fell with resounding thuds. Under the sexton's expert guidance the grave was soon ready. The priest who had officiated at Periathai's funeral conducted a simple ceremony, shaking his head at intervals. I waited for the people to disperse so that I could be by myself.

It was dark when the crowd thinned and the bicycles, motorcycles and cars beside the main road moved. Menon, who had come rather late, perhaps hearing about the fuss Naina made, took me aside.

"You're an educated young man. Advise your father. I'm ready to give him back his job," he said.

Naina was bidding farewell to the people who had come. But he kept glancing towards Menon and me.

"He won't listen," I told Menon.

Karupi, almost a stranger among us, came sniffling up to me as Menon limped away.

"Ravi, talk to your father. Why is he bringing so much shame on us? He did me a favour a long time ago. He made me his wife. Though I still keep the shop, it's for him," she said.

Naina had seen the last of the men off. He came slowly towards us.

"I know what Ayah and you said to him," he said, staring at us.

Then he took out a cigar, something he hadn't done for a long time. We watched him light it and take the first puff. He turned to go, but changed his mind. He faced us again, striking his chest several times.

"I've dignity," he said.

16

As Naina's actions became complex and unpredictable, I was constantly summoned to Bedong. Though he was calm and self-absorbed in the mornings, in the nights he turned violent. The house had its windows and doors shut one night when I dropped in for a casual visit. I reached the door only with the help of lights from the cars passing on the main road.

There was a whispered consultation within the house.

"It's Brother," Samy said.

"Wait, Ravi," Mother called.

"Don't open the door to useless people," Naina warned.

Then two pin-points of light showed through the door. Someone moved behind it, unbolting it. Naina held the door open with one hand; in the other he gripped a parang.

"All sorts of people come to the door nowadays," he said. "I'm glad to see you, Son."

Mother's lips quivered as she stood behind him, watching me. Samy opened the windows and put on the radio. My younger brothers and sisters filled the hall, forming a family again.

"Go back tomorrow," Mother said.

I nodded as it was a holiday the following day. Mother made me a drink in the kitchen.

"Have you seen the things we got from our land?" she called.

I went to the kitchen. The floor was littered with a variety of vegetables, jambus, banana combs and custard apples. She picked two succulent ones from the last pile and put them in my hands.

"You always liked them," she said. "Sit down and drink your tea."

Naina was chattering away in the hall, Samy interrupting him a few times, the other children laughing. Everyone was unnaturally relaxed.

"He has become very strange," Mother said.

"Don't mumble there like two old women!" Naina said. "Come out here!"

"Let Ravi finish his drink!" Mother called, then in a softer voice said, "He always takes the parang to bed. And he has bored holes in the walls."

"I'll talk to him tomorrow," I said softly, though I was angry.

"The government people opened Kumar's grave and took him away," Mother said tearfully.

"You don't bury the dead anywhere you like," I said.

"I don't know what's happening," she said.

"I'm afraid of showing my face anywhere," I said.

The family slept late into the morning. Naina, with his inexhaustible energy, up early, moved about in the prayer room. His chanting woke Mother and the rest. Mother made Naina a glass of milk which would see him through to a midday vegetarian meal. He sat on in the shrine-room. When he came from his contemplation he dressed in shorts and worked in the fields. Around noon he left for the river.

"Go quietly behind him," Mother said. "Usually one of the children accompany him."

I followed Naina at a distance. He carried a copper jar, selected from Periathai's collection. When he reached the river bank he wore a thundu around his waist and stood on a tiny landing he had built over the water. Then, dipping the jar into the river, he poured the water over his body. When he was completely wet he waded into the river until the water reached his waist; he stood there a long time, his hands held parallel to his shoulders, index finger and thumb curled into a zero. His eyes were closed. Then he immersed himself completely and, wading back to the bank, let the sun dry his body.

"The river purifies," he said when he saw me. "No school today?"

He picked up the jar, filled it with water and started for home. He shut himself up in the shrine-room for another hour. Mother had laid out his lunch: rice, dhal curry, *papadam*, on a banana leaf. A silver tumbler of boiled well water stood to the right.

Naina shook his head when he saw the tumbler.

"Unboiled, well water," he said.

"Samy, draw some," Mother said.

We had our meal after Naina finished, and I returned to Sungai Petani, to my books.

Whenever I had the time I went to Bedong. The staff had got word, somehow, that my father had become a sensation in Bedong. They threw me odd glances. Even the men with whom I shared meals at the Chinese stall talked with less passion and skirted certain topics. The parang Naina kept under his pillow worried me.

My fear was justified. Naina had taken to drinking again. When he returned he raged round the house, dashing plates and mugs to the floor. The trunks of Indian lamps, vessels and mats he had acquired, were spilled all over the house. They weren't all Periathai's, some of them being my mother's wedding gifts.

"Don't destroy them," Mother pleaded.

"Useless! Useless!" Naina muttered, momentarily spent.

---

papadam – Flat, spicy wafer served at Indian lunches.

Karupi came that day, loaded with fruits, bottles of Stout and sweets for the children.

"Why did you come?" Naina said. "I'm only a poor man. You like the face of money."

"Bedong is talking," Karupi said. "They say I've forgotten my duty to you."

She turned her face to me, a haggard thin mask. The joy had gone out of her but she was determined to get Naina back to the shop.

"The boys are getting wild without a father," she said.

"You control them well from the money drawer," Naina said.

"Money! Money!" Karupi burst out. "I'm still paying the debts you started."

"Money asks for money, like a ghost asks for blood," Naina said almost gleefully.

"When will you be the man you were? When others obeyed and respected you. Not even a goat will look at you now," Karupi said.

"Better that way," Naina said.

"Have you no sense of duty?" Karupi said.

"To what?" Naina said. "Now go away! When you come I smell dirty money!"

"That's how a lazy, proud man talks," Karupi said, but she left hurriedly.

Karupi's visit had upset him, and my presence didn't calm him down.

"Shut the windows and doors! Put the lights out!" he ordered peremptorily.

"It's still early," I said.

"You don't know the evil eye of the people, son," he said gently. "Only darkness will keep their evil away."

He went to the shrine-room, shut the door, and mumbled prayers in the dark. We assembled in the kitchen and, keeping our voices low, ate our dinner. Even then

Naina called from his room.

"Are you all conspiring? Don't listen to them, listen to me."

Suddenly, in the middle of the night, when we were sleeping, exhausted by the tension, he went round the doors and windows, unbolting and bolting them.

"Go away! We're happy here," he suddenly shouted.

"What's it?" I said, going to him.

"I saw a man," Naina said. "But I frightened him away."

But the Town Council men came the next day. Naina became more agitated. His behaviour was so erratic that I had to go to work from the Bedong house. Sometimes he listened to my commands; sometimes he raved against me. Then for hours he was silent, closetted in the shrine-room. Though he was physically with us, his actions were motivated by an intense, private dream.

In the mornings, after a particularly brutal bout, he worked frenziedly in the fields. He added another furrow, manured and watered the other plots. Body covered with sweat and mud, he returned and slept in the hall, a child abandoned to fatigue. In the afternoon, when tired from watching him I fell into a doze, my mother suddenly shook me.

"He's burning things! Even your books," she said.

I rushed to the back, where my adolescent store, the cupboard from the shop and the crate of books from my English stay stood around a roaring fire. The drawers had been violently prised open and emptied into the fire. My international passport, letters from my pen-pals and some of my earlier certificates were gone! The crate was already broken and half the contents tipped into the fire.

"Don't burn them, Naina!" I said.

"You won't need them," he said quietly.

He flung the larger books, files and papers into the well-stoked flames. But when I moved to retrieve the more valuable of my documents, he thrust me away.

"I'm telling you, these are unnecessary," he said.

His behaviour deteriorated. When I took him to the Sungai Petani hospital, under the pretext that I wanted him to see my rented room, the doctor gave him sedatives and said we could look after him in the house. For a week he was calm and well-behaved. But soon he learned to deceive the doctors. Even if they kept him under observation, he spoke like other men, read most of the time, and didn't object to whatever food he was served.

Back home he went back to his rampages. It was a nightmare for me. I resented his burning my possessions: they meant so much to me. I was tired of his irrational rantings. Once more I stayed back for prolonged periods in Sungai Petani. Then Samy came and I had to return.

He had lost touch with reality completely. Now he not only increased his visits to the river, but he also brought pebbles, clay and lallang to the house. These he laid out on a banana leaf before Nataraja.

"Breathe your spirit into them!" he chanted. "Make them the clay and grass of my body!"

The house filled with incense smoke and camphor smells. He forced my mother to clean the house at least twice a day. The ritual vessels had to be spotless. But in the evenings he would roll up his bed clothes and pillow in a mat and, shouldering it, walk towards the road. He stood on the grass verge, looking at the cars (some passengers made filthy signs at him), and returned rather disconsolate to the house.

"I've gone round the world," he said. "But I always have to come back."

It became more painful for me to visit the house.

When I returned, after an absence of a fortnight, he immediately made me sit beside him and listen to him.

"We've done our best, Ravi," he rambled. "I've spoken

to Gandhi and Nehru. See this thundu? Mahatma wove it for me at his wheel. And Nehru said, 'Why didn't you come to me before?' I said I had no time. Working for my wives and children!"

He was silent for a while. Then he looked out of the hall door as if he saw something I didn't, chuckling.

"I told Mahatma about my latest car. 'Not only white men drive in cars nowadays,' the Mahatma said. He touched his body as if remembering the wounds he had received when thrown out of the train in the other country. 'You've done well,' he said. But Nehru didn't smile. He said, 'Go away!' "

"Time for you to pray," Mother said, embarrassed at Naina's inflated talk.

Naina silently obeyed but his stay in the closed room was brief. He came back smiling and confident of himself.

"Don't think only you know things," he said, falling back into his talkative mood, "because you went to England. I played golf with the Tunku the other day. He told me not to worry. Everything would be all right."

Mother gave him tea and his pills and he slumped into a deep sleep. We had to carry him to his room and stretch him out on the mat he slept on at the foot of Nataraja's statue.

17

Naina's last action, coming after he had stopped raving, shocked us. The house filled with a pleasurable silence when he worked in the fields. My presence, when he bathed in the river and stood in the sunlight, didn't bother him. A deep silence settled on his face. He was thinner but not weak. He always brought back a load of objects to the shrine-room. A tree trunk, swathes of lallang, clumps of grass, bank clay shaped into a hut, were presented to Nataraja, under thick, incense smoke. Periathai's lamps and ritual vessels were put away.

"You've always used them," Mother protested.

"They are useless now," Naina said.

He fashioned his own urns, lamps, jars, and statues with many arms and faces, out of the clay he brought from the river. Sitting on the mat he had woven from lallang and wild reeds that grew near the river, he began to chant in a garbled language. It embarrassed me to hear him recite a rhythm mounted on Tamil, Malay and even Chinese words. It was a secret language, like the one we invented among ourselves when we were adolescents (driven by some frenzy for ritual privacy), with additional consonants or dropped vowels. He destroyed the trunks Periathai and he had acquired, but the Nataraja statue, he retained.

The Town Council men came but he was always polite to them.

"We'll go away soon, Ayah," he said.

They trudged back to the main road, pacified.

Naina came into the hall whenever I returned, left the shrine-room open as a tacit invitation, and resumed his contemplation and prayers. Sitting there among the bits of trees, plants and his clay vessels, he was a man possessed by a special, esoteric dream. That was the last time I saw him alive.

When I came, summoned by Samy, the house was a mass of burnt rubble. People stood at the roadside, pointing and chattering away. My mother had refused to leave the charred site; a tent had been rigged up for her. She sat on the ground, clutching the last boy to her breast.

"Look at what he has done to himself!" she wailed, beat her breasts, and screamed, the minute she saw me.

I gazed at her, searching for words to console her. I was relieved when one of the Town Council men approached me.

"Come and keep an eye on the things," he said.

Most of the clothes, books and pictures were completely burnt. The warped, paintless plates, a cracked mug and some pots were littered where the kitchen had stood. The articles in the shrine-room had fared better. Nataraja, only darker, had fallen on his side. Periathai's tier lamps had survived the flames, one or two twisted by the heat. A cordon ran round the shrine-room so that spectators wouldn't step on the ashes.

The priest had come and he had helped the other men rake the ashes for the bones. He put them and a little of the white ash in a new, clay pot.

Naina received a simple funeral. We accompanied the priest to the river, I carrying the remains in that pot. My brothers were dressed in white; the priest made us bathe in the water, then called us to the bank.

While we had been dipping ourselves in the water he had built a model house, with four doors, on the tiny landing. It was a remarkable piece of design, complete with kitchen and bedroom. Naina was represented by a tar effigy lying on a tiny bed, covered by a small piece of white cloth.

We, the sons, anointed him with oil and herbal paste, poured the symbolic pail of water on him. The priest opened each of the doors in turn. When the last was removed we walked round Naina without looking at him.

"Now go away a few yards," the priest said.

Our other relatives scattered the ashes and bones into the river.

"Now he is part of the water and soil of the earth," the priest said loudly.

But I had not walked away from Naina, or Periathai, for they were still vividly in my mind. With difficulty and uncertainty, I wrote the following poem, containing an immature and tormenting recognition:

Full Circle
(for Naina)

Have you been lost
for words?

Have you been lost
for words when
you had them stacked
like images in a dream?

Have you been lost for words
when they imprisoned
your flesh, your thoughts,
feelings that rose with the wind?

Have you been lost?

Then words will not serve.
They will be like the culture
you refused at adolescence,
drinking from the tap
instead of the well.

The dregs at the bottom
of well water is the ash
of family prayers you rejected.
The clay taste
the deep-rootedness
you turned aside from –
for the cleanliness of chlorine.

Words will not serve.

You'll be twisted by them
into nameless little impulses
that roam dark city roads, raging.
They will be vague knots
of feelings, lustreless, cultureless,
buried in a heart that will not serve.

LINGUISTIC BOUNDARIES:
K.S. MANIAM'S THE RETURN

By

Dr. Anne Brewster

Centre For Studies In Australian Literature
Curtin University of Technology at Perth

K.S. MANIAM'S autobiographical novel *The Return* opens
with a description of the narrator's grandmother's arrival in
Malaysia with her baggage and three sons. The old woman,
addressed by the honorific 'Periathai', is tenacious and
resourceful in starting life anew with her family in a strange
land; she works first as a tinker, then as a healer before
settling down to farm the land and sell her produce. This
tenacity and resourcefulness are, in the narrator's eyes,
products of her 'Indian skills and heritage';[1] she draws her
vitality from cultural wisdom and experience and as such is
a link to a tradition that is receding from the narrator.
Listening to his grandmother's stories the narrator muses
poignantly: 'I felt I stood on the edge of a world I may have
known' (p.6). The novel, in its first chapter, would appear
to embark upon a biography of this remarkable woman. In
the succeeding chapters, however, another figure assumes
the focal position of authority in the young boy's life: his
father.

Kannan, the narrator's father, is a complex character,
neurotic or capable and industrious by turn; one thing
becomes clear, however; Kannan, like his son, looks to
Periathai for confirmation of tradition. And because Periathai

---

[1] K.S. Maniam *The Return* (Kuala Lumpur: Heinemann Asia, 1981), p.3. All
subsequent quotations will be included as page numbers in the text.

herself came from a farming community, this tradition is expressed by both her and her son in the desire to own land and to build on it. In the generations preceding Ravi, the narrator, this family is doomed to failure. Periathai never got to own the house and land where she had lived for many years; she died disappointed, 'speechless' and without a 'farewell'. And history repeated itself; Kannan spent the last remaining years of his life obsessively seeking ownership of the land on which he lived: 'we can make all the money, get all the learning. But these are useless if our house pillars don't sink into the clay of the land' (p.167), he tells his son, Ravi.

In the years preceding his father's death, however, the narrator had become detached from his father's and Periathai's dream of owning land:

> I stood outside Periathai's and Naina's [his father's] preoccupations. Their imagination couldn't grasp the real complexity that surrounded us. I had, watching Periathai's failure to earn a home in this land, decided to acquire a skill that would allow me a comfortable, unthreatened existence. One's world was, after all, private...A mild anger filled me as I saw Periathai die homeless. But I considered hers an irrational attitude. No one would compel me into sharing another, immature ambition.
>
> Only my studies mattered. I was at them constantly, aware that I could go to England if I won a teaching bursary. Naina's interests and my family's struggles became unimportant. The dignity of the individual was the only thing that engaged me. (pp.147/8)

In two generations, then, the dream of the immigrant Indian

in Malaysia to 'drive some stake into the country' (p.147) had transmuted. Ravi, a representative of the first Malaysian-born generation, saw the 'complexity' of the immigrant community from a different perspective. Its traditional communal lifestyle held little appeal for him. Rather than fight to put down roots in the land, he retreated into a 'private' world and decided to pursue the 'dignity of the individual' by other means. The only way to obtain this in his eyes was through the acquisition of 'a skill' that would make him socially mobile, and that skill was education. And education in colonial Malaysia entailed the adoption of the colonial language, English. Maniam's introduction to English proved to be a major cultural occurrence: it was to be the language of his autobiographical novel.

The Russian linguist and literary critic Mikhail Bakhtin was particularly interested in the evolution of literary forms within multilingual communities. He coined the term 'polyglossia' to describe 'the simultaneous presence of two or more national languages operating within a single cultural system'. Polyglossia, he goes on to say, relativises language:

> Where languages and cultures interanimate each other, language became something entirely different, its very nature changes: in place of a single, unitary sealed-off Ptolemaic world of language, there appeared the open Galilean world of many languages, mutually animating each other.[2]

The movement of a speech community or an individual from monoglossia to polyglossia is an important one in which two myths perish: 'the myth of a language that

---

[2]Mikhail Bakhtin, *The Dialogic Imagination,* ed. M. Holquist, trans. C. Emerson and M. Holquist (Austin: University of Texas Press, 1981), p.65.

presumes to be the only language, and the myth of a language that presumes to be completely unified'.[3] Certain literary genres such as epic, myth and tragedy, Bakhtin argues, are products of the centralising force of monoglossia. Polyglossia, on the other hand, which opens up the possibility of many different 'voices' in the text, gives rise to the genre of the novel. He defines the novel as being characterised by 'a diversity of social speech types (sometimes even diversity of languages) and a diversity of individual voices, artistically organised'.[4] These 'voices' manifest within the text in 'authorial speech', 'the speeches of narrators' and 'the speech of characters'. Bakhtin argues that the Roman Empire and the Renaissance, for example, were both periods of polyglossia in which novelistic genres emerged. He goes on to suggest that this diversity of voices in the novel is its characteristic feature which he labels 'heteroglossia'. Heteroglossia, he says, endows the novel with a dialogic quality: the multiplicity of voices therein are engaged in an internal 'dialogue' with each other. Because these voices are drawn from various socially stratified discourses the novel is the site of 'struggle among socio-linguistic points of view'.[5]

Bakhtin's comments are especially relevant to post-colonial discourse. Here we can immediately distinguish at least two different 'voices' operating within the text: the discursive strategies of the European tradition and the dialogic voice of the post-colonial writer who reinterprets or rewrites this tradition from his or her own perspective. Post-colonial autobiography as a genre takes on particular significance in this context. It is a discourse that places the post-colonial writer as the first-person subject of what had

---

[3]Ibid., p.68.
[4]Ibid., p.262.
[5]Ibid., p.273.

been the coloniser's language. It empowers the individual to speak on his or her own behalf where formerly he or she had been spoken for by others. I would like to pick up this idea of the individual being empowered to speak against authority, because *The Return* seems to me to be very much concerned with the struggle against authority. I would like to propose that the writer here challenges or undermines various authoritative 'voices' acting within and upon his discourse.

The first is the voice of colonialism manifested in the novel in the discourse of Miss Nancy, the young Ravi's school teacher. The second voice is that of Mr. Menon, the superintendent of the hospital compound where Ravi's family lives. Menon's discourse, like that of Miss Nancy smacks of domination, but here the domination is socio-economic, that of class struggle. The third voice of authority against which Ravi struggles, is Oedipal, that of his father, Kannan.

Each of these three authoritative voices is positioned within the polyglossic or multilingual context of the novel. Both Miss Nancy and Menon function within the hierarchy established by colonialism and impose their authority through a privileged access to 'proper' English. The struggle between Ravi and his father, on the other hand, positions the autobiographical subject in a dialogic relationship with his 'mother' or should I say 'father' tongue. The outcome of this Oedipal struggle is the father's eventual refuge in a private multilingual language.

I will now consider briefly each of these three dialogic encounters in the narrative. We notice that those passages in the novel that deal with Miss Nancy are characterised by both confession and a counter-discourse to the authority Miss Nancy represents – a counter-discourse of authorial satire which indicates the empowerment of the post-colonial speaking subject. The humiliation of the young Ravi at the hands of his teacher is amply avenged by the cutting satire of the adult narrator. The traditional English fairy tales with which Miss Nancy woos her class are re-read by the narrator as myths of power and desire that expose Miss Nancy's sexual and colonial predatoriness. Miss Nancy's bright young disciple here makes over the language by dismantling and deconstructing the colonial discursive strategies inherent in it.

If Miss Nancy is a representative of the colonial authority, another figure of authority who oppresses Ravi is Mr. Menon, the superintendent of the hospital compound. The 'class prejudice' of the hospital workers' hierarchy is cause for constant friction for the lower members of the pecking order. Ravi's relationship with Mr. Menon is one of continually reiterated submission. He records the frequent rituals of humiliation that he suffers at Menon's hands, the major one being the confirmation of his role as a launderer. 'You're only good for washing other people's dirty clothes' (p.43), Menon tells him on one occasion. Significantly, one of the privileges Menon claims over his workers is the use of English, and Ravi's progress at school usurps this authority. Menon takes Ravi to task over his proficiency in English: 'I heard you can speak the white man's language better than my son' (p.43), he challenges. English was the language of the hospital elite and for this reason its use was guarded jealously. Ravi relates that:

> The language we spoke in the long verandah of the houses was a defiant version of English, mingled with and sounding very Tamil. The minute we broke into 'pure' English we were scolded.
>
> 'You'll have Ayah's anger on our heads!'
>
> But English, as spoken by our teachers in schools, reigned supreme among the more skilled, educated personnel of this estate hospital. (p.80)

Menon establishes his position in the colonial hierarchy and jealously guards access to the main instrument of power of that authority, the English language. But Ravi is to turn Menon's instrument of power against him and escape from the compound altogether.

Perhaps the most complex figure of authority in the novel, however, is Ravi's father. As mentioned earlier, Kannan dominates Ravi's early life and childhood, and despite his occasional outbursts of melancholy or neuroticism, is generally responsible and resourceful in raising his family. In the last section of the novel, which deals with Ravi's return from his two-year sojourn in England, however, Ravi's relationship with his father undergoes a dramatic change. This change is heralded by Ravi's first meeting with his father on his return, where he describes him as being like 'a small child, ill-treated and lost'.(p.160) Ironically, Ravi's return is not the joyous homecoming of the prodigal son but the reluctant return of a disaffected and deracinated adult. The bitterness and poignancy of this episode with its depiction of the father's Oedipal demise, heralds the approaching end of the narrative. This section of the text more than any other takes on a consistently confessional tone as the narrator gives expression to his resentment, guilt, anger and grief. Father and son are locked in an Oedipal struggle. Just as Ravi despises his father's 'irrational' and 'obsessive' dream of acquiring a house and land, so Kannan comes to regret the authority Ravi's English education has given him; he burns his son's books and letters. Ravi's 'success' within the post-colonial system is read here against Kannan's decline. And if Ravi's story is about the findings of a language and a voice then his father's story describes the loss or disintegration of a language and a voice. Ultimately, like his mother he dies 'speechless' and 'without a farewell'. As his sanity crumbles he speaks in riddles and secrets; his discourse is cryptic and laced with lies and tall tales. He resorts to a 'secret' and 'garbled' nonsense language which the narrator describes as:

> a rhythm mounted on Tamil, Malay and even Chinese words. It was a secret language, like the one we invented among ourselves when we were adolescents (driven by some frenzy for ritual privacy), with additional consonants and dropped vowels. (p.180)

This private multilingual language could be described as glossolalia, the deranged speech associated with schizophrenic disorders. Julia Kristeva's discussion of glossolalia[6] would seem relevant at this point. She defines glossolalia as an irrational outburst of pre-linguistic rhythmic utterance that challenges the symbolic order imposed, in this case, by the authoritative discourse of 'proper' English. Kannan's language can thus be read as oppositional to the acquired language of his son.

The autobiographical narrator then, in the various stages of acquiring English has been engaged in a dialogue with authority. Ironically, however, the acquisition of English, the language of authority, marginalises the narrator within his own ethnic community; he is estranged from his father and his schoolboy peers who call him 'white monkey'. His father's multilingual glossolalia serves to remind us that the autobiographical subject is not simply straddling two languages, English and Tamil, nor simply two cultures, that of the coloniser and the colonised, the oppresser and the oppressed. The multi-ethnic community in which the narrative is set makes the situation far more complex; simple binary oppositions break down. A parallel

---

[6]Julia Kristeva, *Desire in Language*, (Oxford: Basil Blackwell, 1980), p.133.

situation can be found in Fiji. Writing of the Fijian Indians, for example, Mark Williams says:

> the Indians occupy the crucial and anxious
> position between the racial groups in Fiji who
> obviously wear the marks, 'oppressor' and
> 'oppressed'. They find themselves in the
> untenable middle ground...[7]

It is the portrayal of this 'untenable middle ground' that lends the novel its poignancy and complexity. Its title, *The Return,* would suggest the desire to re-establish racial and ethnic origins but this nostalgia is mixed with a sober realisation of the impossibility of this quest; his grandmother's world is beyond Ravi's reach. The ethnicity of the immigrant is further problematised in the multicultural context of Malaysia where nationalism is defined in terms of race, in this case, the Malays. Because only literature written in Malay is defined as National literature, writing in other languages such as English is seen to exist outside the categorisation 'national'.

The implications of this are far-reaching. Immigrant groups, because of the very nature of their status, challenge the concept of a homogeneous community. They also challenge and undermine the concept of racial purity and originality: Homi Bhabha has brilliantly analysed racism in psychological terms as analogous to castration fear[8] - the fear of the other who invalidates one's sense of oneself as the prototype human being. Nationalism is a construct which characterises a community as being distinguished by

---

[7]Mark Williams, 'The Anxiety of Writing: Language and Belonging in New Zealand and Fiji', *Span* 22, p.95.

[8]Homi K. Bhabha, 'Difference, Discrimination and the Discourse of Colonialism', *The Politics of Theory,* ed. Francis Barker et al., (Colchester: University of Essex Press), 1983.

some apparently essential, natural or absolute quality (for example, race) that in turn relegates outsiders or exiles to a position of otherness or inferiority. But even concepts of race and ethnicity are themselves constructs and metaphors (are any of us here actually black, white or yellow?) The juxtaposition of different cultures demonstrates the arbitrariness of nationalism that it is merely, in Edward Said's words, 'a history selectively strung together in a narrative form'.[9] Said goes on to say that for the exile or immigrant, the 'new world' they enter seems initially 'unreal' and that this 'unreality resembles fiction'. The immigrant, he suggests, is thus naturally disposed to novel writing, because what fiction itself does is to demonstrate that 'other worlds may exist'. This is perhaps why the young Ravi compulsively reads everything he can lay his hands on and finds a particular delight in entering the 'liberating' world of cartoon and comic book characters. He describes how this then gives him the ability to 'read' the people in the world around him as caricatures, especially those that threaten him; 'Ratnam seemed such a poor joke of a man; the Ayah a robot, easily shortcircuited, of power' (p.93). In reading the world around him as fiction, the novelist, the immigrant subject empowers himself; he is constructing his own world.

Mikhail Bakhtin's comments again come to mind here; within the multilingual environment of Malaysia, the heteroglossia of the novel challenges the so-called authority of any monoglotic or monolingual tradition. A novel like *The Return* thus works to deconstruct the dominant discourses of the milieu, in this case, that of the Colonial language and its literary tradition (as demonstrated by the satirising of Miss Nancy) and that of nationalism. Emerging as it does from the 'boundary line between cultures and languages' the novel is inevitably heteroglossic and combats what Bakhtin sees as

---

[9]Edward Said, 'Reflections on Exile', *Granta* 13, pp.159/172.

the particularly national unity of monoglossia. The blurb on
the back cover of *The Return,* for example, informs us that
the novel 'reveals how an immigrant population comes or
does not come to terms with a common nationality'. The
ambiguity of this statement deconstructs itself; an immigrant
population in the ambiguous position of what Lloyd
Fernando has described as experiencing 'the fear of losing
[its] identity on the one hand, and on the other the fear that
[it] may not succeed in achieving the new identity which [it]
seeks to assume,[10] is hardly able to participate in a
'common' or shared nationality. 'The boundary line between
cultures and languages', then, to repeat Bakhtin's phrase, is
the site of the 'creating consciousness'. And perhaps what
this consciousness reveals is that all boundaries are, in the
last analysis, fictional.

     Anne Brewster teaches at Curtin University at Perth,
Australia. She has a book on Malaysian/Singaporean Literature in
English coming out with The Singapore University Press and
another on Postcolonial Literatures with Melbourne Unviersity
Press.

---

[10]Lloyd Fernando, *Cultures in Conflict,* (Singapore: Graham Brash, 1986),
    p.13.

This study was previously published in 'A Sense of Exile': Essays in the
    Literature of the Asia-Pacific Region (Nedlands: The Centre for Studies in
    Australian Literature, Dept. of English, The University of Western
    Australia, 1988) With their kind permission.

K.S. MANIAM
In A Far Country
The New Novel
Forthcoming 31st Aug. 1993, P'bk. U.K. Price GBP £5.99

The protagonist, Rajan, disillusioned with the trappings of silk and satin, reflects on his unrelenting past and old companions. In trying to recant a persona of attachment to material progress, he discovers self-apprehension in an authentic identity.

What was he? The question obsessed me for a long time. But as I went on watching I understood only a little of what he was and wanted to be. He became such a focus of attention for me that I kept, in writing, a study of his movements, behaviour and final developments in his life. I'll reproduce it here so as to see if it can throw any light on my present predicament. The language appears stilted and pseudo-scientific but that was what I was at that time. I've tried to keep myself as much as possible out of the account. Sometimes I've written as I followed his behaviour; sometimes I've written in recollection. This record is extensive in the beginning when we hardly talked; it comes to an abrupt end just before he met his death.

The Lee Shin Study

This study attempts to understand, in detail, Lee Shin's behaviour, thoughts and motivation. While it cannot be exhaustive, it can, nevertheless, be an honest record of what was seen, heard and observed. In this place, after work is done, there is more than enough time for such activities.

Men can be put into two categories: the independent and the dependent. Lee Shin is an independent. The other men here mass together: in the mess, coffeeshops, rest house and the houses of nurses and salesgirls. They clearly belong to the second group. Their code of ethics is based on mutual support. Thus, they support each other's opinions, attitudes, idiosyncracies, actions and the ability to put down those outside their circle.

Lee Shin seems to have come to the settlement with a fierce desire to safe-guard his freedom. From the beginning he has kept to himself as if he mistrusted people. It has been more than a month since Lee Shin came under observation but he has not said a word to the observer. As a neighbour, he is uncommunicative and sits by himself in the verandah, late into the evening. Now and then he whistles a tune which has no resemblance to any that the observer has heard. Sometimes the whistling rises to such a pitch as to sound inhuman. Then he breaks off suddenly.

No sound comes from his house throughout the late afternoon. When the observer wakes up from his nap, the house next door is still quiet and looks uninhabited. The observer who has had lunch in town and is preparing to go out for his tea, wonders what Lee Shin has eaten for the afternoon meal.

When the observer returns from his tea, he finds Lee Shin dressed in white shorts and T-shirt. He is out on the slope of grass beside his house ready to begin his exercises. This is the part of Lee Shin's behaviour that the observer finds strange. He never carries out any of the regular exercises young men pick up. Instead, he creates a slow-paced pantomime with his trunk, hands and legs.

Sometimes his movements are so painfully slow that the observer wonders if Lee Shin has entered some sort of a trance. There he stands, within an invisible centre, his body defying gravity and the backbone's flexibility, arms stretched out in a kind of farewell. Then he bends low and holds himself temptingly between sinking down to rest and rising up to fierce combat. But he does neither. He just remains in that position for a long time. He is rivetted to the earth and sky with an invisible bolt. To the casual onlooker he may be a bronze statue balancing itself between life and death.

Perhaps it was that moment that had attracted the observer's attention to this lonely individual. Lee Shin then lifts himself up as if by the hair. The head goes up, followed by his shoulders, waist and thigh, all in slow motion. He does something with his shoulder blades and they spread out like a cobra's hood poised for attack. He dips his head and brings up his hands so that the fingers curve rigidly, as if they were the snake's fangs. He advances slowly, and the fangs come down viciously on some invisible enemy. Lee Shin straightens, relaxes, and resuming his usual slouch, whistles his way to the verandah and sits down on the steps.

The evening is mildly warm and Lee Shin remains seated there for some time, almost immobile. As the day recedes, he acquires the dimension of a granite statue. His body, carved up by shadow and light, appears to be supported by an emaciated purpose. There is dignity in that posture but little else.

When the observer returns from his evening meal, Lee Shin

has already bathed and changed. He is once again seated in the verandah, on a chair, and he has started something new. There is a bright object in his hands; he polishes it with a yellow, velvety cloth. Then Lee Shin puts the shiny object to his lips and the sound it emits confuses the observer for a while and then only amuses him. As Lee Shin launches into a full melody, the observer becomes more and more disoriented. He has never heard a harmonica produce such strange strains. 'Yankee Doodle' comes to his mind for that was what was traditionally played on that instrument or it was 'My Bonnie Lies Over the Ocean'.

The days now are a torment for the observer for he does not know how to stop Lee Shin from playing the harmonica. On the silent grounds of the settlement, the music from the harmonica booms like some unearthly sound. What restrains the observer, however, is the objective he chose when he undertook this study. Once he interferes, the subject will be robbed of his peculiar habits and personal circumstances. So the observer has to bear his discomfort and adopt the attitude of a detached recorder.

As the days pass, Lee Shin plays furiously but stops now and then to look in the direction of the observer's house. In the company's offices he casts shy but significant glances at the observer. Is some change imminent in Lee Shin?

The past three days the harmonica has been reedy, desultory and cautious. No blaring, pungent thrusts come to provoke; instead, Lee Shin looks more and more towards the observer's house. The attitude of the other personnel is becoming clearer and is, sometimes, distressing. Obviously, they would like to be elsewhere, in some of the brighter towns but the money here is good. Perhaps this recognition makes them quieter but beneath the calm lies a latent viciousness.

All this makes the observer view Lee Shin differently. He is so self-contained nothing seems to touch him. Can the observer be affected by the observed? It is certainly so in this case: Lee Shin's self-sufficient existence gives the observer a strange sense of confidence. Some of the restlessness the observer felt earlier is gone.

Some weekends Lee Shin tramps off into the jungle nearby, haversack on his back and a butterfly net in his hand. Returning in the evening, he sits in the hall and mounts the specimens. The observer sees him bent over the butterflies, the syringe in his fingers sucking out the insides and, later, pumping in the formaldehyde. What is there about the posture that says neither the activity nor the interest will last? Two or three weeks later Lee Shin has shifted his attention elsewhere. He has taken to pressing leaves, flowers and rare plants. Then he is back at the verandah railing, barehanded and listless.

Then one evening he signals to the observer. It is not so much an invitation as a command, the hand waving imperatively. The observer, taken aback, wonders whether to comply or not. But he is curious and crosses the short distance to Lee Shin's house.

The observer mounts the steps and stands beside Lee Shin. The man makes no move to acknowledge or greet him. Lee Shin's gaze is still turned towards the house down the slope as if the observer has not left it. Then, suddenly, he snaps out of his reverie and looks at the observer.

"The harmonica music has brought you here," Lee Shin says.

"In a way," I say.

The power and necessity to tell a story is the original impulse of any fiction. Rajan, Zulkifli, Lee Shin, Sivasurian and Santhi of different race and religion contribute to the cosmos of this convergent world In A Far Country.